THE SHINING BRIDGE

Charles Ashton has lived most of his life in Scotland and recently moved back to the village where he was brought up. His books for young people include The Dragon Fire Trilogy, *Jet Smoke and Dragon Fire* (shortlisted for both the Guardian Fiction Award and the W H Smith Mind Boggling Books Award), *Into The Spiral* and *The Shining Bridge,* as well as another novel, *Billy's Drift,* and two stories for younger readers *Ruth and The Blue Horse* and *The Giant's Boot* (shortlisted for the 1995 Smarties Book Prize). "Why do I write?" he says. "Well, why do I start to go to pieces after a year or two of doing anything else? If I have to 'go out' and look for a job now, the first thing I shall have to tell my prospective employer is that I am unreliable – take me on at your own risk." He is married with five children and a variety of animals.

Also by Charles Ashton

Into the Spiral
Jet Smoke and Dragon Fire

THE
SHINING
BRIDGE

CHARLES ASHTON

WALKER BOOKS
AND SUBSIDIARIES
LONDON · BOSTON · SYDNEY

First published 1993 by Walker Books Ltd
87 Vauxhall Walk, London SE11 5HJ

This edition published 1996

2 4 6 8 10 9 7 5 3 1

Text © 1993 Charles Ashton
Cover illustration © 1996 Julek Heller

The right of Charles Ashton to be identified as
author of this work has been asserted by him in accordance
with the Copyright, Designs and Patents Act 1988.

Printed in England

British Library Cataloguing in Publication Data
A catalogue record for this book is available
from the British Library.

ISBN 0-7445-4743-1

For
Rachel

CONTENTS

1

THE QUIET STREET

In a way, being friends with Pats made up to Trina for not having Max any more. Not that Pats was a dog, but he could be very dog-like. Sometimes the three of them – Pats, Pats' father and Trina – would go for walks together, and Pats would run after sticks and fetch them back – except that he would throw them first as well.

"I wish we could get another dog," Trina told Pats' father.

"Can't you?" he said.

"Not now that Mum's working," Trina replied glumly.

"Don't you like her having a job?"

Trina shook her head, sighed. "I don't know. It's all since Kitty – went. The job takes her mind off things. But nothing's the same any more. I like Newborough though. I'm glad we came here."

She hadn't been to begin with. It was all another crackpot idea of her father's, as far as she was concerned. He had wanted them to move away from the city after the riots. "There's going to be more – this is just the start of it," he had said, in his darkest prophet-of-doom voice. And then Max had been run over. Max would have liked it at Newborough; all the places to go, round the edge of the little town.

Now they had got a cat, called Cat; they had moved to Newborough, and things had got better. But then new troubles seemed to begin. Trina wasn't sure how it had happened. Her mother said it was just a stage she was going through; to Trina it seemed her mother was just always finding fault. "Why is it you can't spell properly? Don't they teach you to spell here?" Or, "Don't you ever read the instructions on things?" Or, "Why are you so disorganized?"

And though it was never said, Trina soon began to realize that, somehow, Kitty was always at the back of it: Kitty had been an excellent speller; Kitty had always read instructions and thought everything out before she did something; Kitty was always making lists and never forgot anything and was never late... "Pooh," Trina would mutter to the silence of her room, "Kitty must have been some kind of angel; no wonder she got killed. This world probably wasn't good enough for her."

She no longer had a very clear memory of this perfect older sister; but she did have a memory of the day Kitty went missing. She remembered the feeling of waiting at the airport; waiting and waiting; telephone calls to the uncle and aunt Kitty had been staying with; her father going off to make enquiries; no one seeming to know what was going on, but making up hopeful-sounding stories; and then at last the awful truth dawning, when the world seemed to stop and a huge silence seemed to fall. The aeroplane had simply disappeared. Somewhere in the empty miles of ocean it must have gone down. People tried for months to find it, but there was not a trace: nothing.

There was another memory Trina had, of the time just before they had come to Newborough. Her father had a job for nine months at a university in a town about an hour's drive from the mountains, and one day Trina and her mother had gone for a long walk into these mountains. In a lonely place near a great waterfall they had met Kitty. They didn't see where she had come from, and she was dressed in old-fashioned, rough clothes, and there was a boy with her dressed the same way. The boy had saved her, Kitty explained, and they felt wonderfully grateful to him, but Max growled every time the boy looked at him, as they sat on a rock and ate sandwiches together. They were living, Kitty said, in a place where everything was very old-

11

fashioned and quiet; there were no cars or shops or cities; there were telephones and televisions and an old railway, but none of them worked; there was no electricity. Kitty loved it, but she still wanted to come back home and see everyone – that was why she and the boy had set off to try and find the way back.

It was all too wonderful, but by the next day Trina's mother had forgotten all about it. When Trina tried to remind her, she told her it must have been a dream. At first Trina was certain it hadn't been, but when she found she had no idea where Kitty and the boy had got to, she had to agree that her mother was right. Kitty had told them the boy's name, but Trina couldn't remember that properly either: it was something to do with a bird, which was why she thought it was probably Robin. But she couldn't be sure.

She talked with Pats' father about dreaming. He wrote books, and he liked dreams. "It can be difficult to tell dreams apart from real life," he said. "I keep on having a dream that Pats comes and stands in my bedroom when I'm in bed, and we hold long conversations. I suppose it's a dream, because I know he's never spoken and probably never will – but how can I be sure?"

Their new home was on the edge of Newborough. There was a park opposite, which

Trina liked to look out over when she got up in the mornings, though she didn't care for it later in the day when it was full of boys playing football. Another favourite place was the bridge between the two halves of Newborough. It was called the Union Bridge, and she liked to hang over its parapet and watch the brown water swirling round its stone piers.

A little way up the broad, straight street into the old half of the town (Trina lived in the new half), was the house where Pats lived with his father; and not far beyond that was the small Square of the old town, with its fine houses and its spacious feel. At the Square, the main road was met by the road from Market Glass, which was the way she and Pats and his father took whenever they went for a walk.

One of the buildings in the Square was a tall, narrow house with quaint arched windows, and next to this was the start of a small road.

From the very first moment she saw it, Trina knew there was something special about that road. Something inviting; something odd. It was narrow, and it was cobbled – its cobbles shining dully as if polished by centuries of long-vanished horses' hoofs. There were no windows in the walls of the buildings on either side of it, and it had no pavements. It ambled off at an angle, then turned a corner as if it were starting to try to get back to the Market Glass road.

The first time Trina noticed it was on a still day in April. It was one of those April days that seem as warm and as close as summer, with hazy clouds stretched across a dreamy blue sky. Half a dozen dogs and cats lay stretched on the pavements of the Square, and old ladies in cardigans sweated by, complaining of the heat. But in the entrance to the cobbled road a slight, chill breeze shifted, and Trina was caught by the sigh of it, and the faintest of faint sounds that was like music far away. Something in the pit of her stomach turned over; it was as though she had been wandering in a desert and suddenly got caught in a shower of silver rain.

Strangely, she felt reluctant to go down the little road. "Some time," she murmured to herself, knowing only that "some time" meant "not yet". The feeling grew in her that if once she ventured down there, she would set in motion a chain of events she could never undo.

"Where does that road go?" she asked Pats' father, as the three of them were setting off, as usual, on the road to Market Glass.

"Oh, it's a road to a farm," Pats' father said. "An old place. No one lives there now. The old branch of the railway used to go down that way – the one that the mystery was all about."

"What mystery?"

"What! You haven't heard about the Newborough mystery? It's quite famous. It was

14

when they were sending children away from the cities during the War because of the air raids. A train of evacuee children came out this way, took the branch line at Newborough Junction – and disappeared. It was never heard of again."

Trina shivered.

There was a fall of snow in the middle of April, but it didn't last long. When it had melted from the ditches, the spring began in earnest; grass and trees sprouted, dandelions opened like miniature suns along the edges of walls, and the fields around the town were full of the sound of bleating lambs.

Then came a Saturday morning at the end of April. Trina's father had promised her a trip to the city; it was actually to see some ancient Burial Ship he had dug up and was very excited about. This didn't interest Trina much, though she thought there would be a chance to get to the shops as well. But something came up at the last moment which meant they couldn't go.

"Next weekend, I promise," her father said.

Trina hung over the parapet of the Union Bridge, staring at the brown water below. She felt near to tears, and when she thought about it she realized that this wasn't because of missing the shops, but simply because there were so few times when she was able to do things together with her father. And since they had come to Newborough, fewer and fewer…

She went on up the street, but didn't stop at Pats' house. She came to the Square. There was a brisk wind, with white clouds racing overhead. She paused beside the tall house, but the wind caught her and blew her against its wall. The sun came out from behind a cloud and blinded her. Quickly she turned into the shadow round the side of the house, and stood on the cobbles of the quiet street.

There was no wind here. There was only the slight, shifting breeze – chill on a warm day, gentle and soothing in this rougher weather. And in the sigh of the breeze, faint and far away, the ghost of a tune on a pipe. Almost despite herself, Trina's feet moved off over the cobbles. Ten … twenty … thirty steps. She was round the corner and out of sight of the Square.

The cobbles stopped at the last building on the street; but the road continued as a stony track. Trina walked on. She could see the line of the road to Market Glass, studded with hawthorns and green elders. She could see the line of the old railway coming out of the Cottage Wood, and the ruined farmhouse. The track wasn't leading anywhere near it. Then she stopped, for she saw something she had never seen before.

It was a hill. A small, green-grown hill, almost a perfect pyramid, which had not been there before. It couldn't be mistaken – in the rolling, soft countryside its shape stood out distinctly. Trina stared; then turned, and began to walk quickly homewards, back over the cobbles. She found she was stepping with deliberate calmness, almost as though she were trying not to panic.

2

DREAM FRIENDS

The building site was a strangely quiet island in the midst of the city hubbub. A wall of wooden boards separated it from the street. It was a great square pit of clay full of leaking grey puddles and mounds of rubble; in a far corner a large mechanical digger crouching like a sorrowful yellow spider; and a crane towering overhead, its huge jib pointing like an arm across the site. There was no movement, no activity; work had been stopped.

The dark timbers of the ancient Burial Ship lay in a pattern like a fish's bones near one edge of the pit, with the soil carefully dug away round them and piled to one side – darker, crumbly soil, not the stiff beige clay of the rest of the site.

"It's only a couple of miles from here to the docks," Trina's father said. "It was probably dragged here from the sea on rollers and then buried." He gazed proudly at his find. "The prow's missing, that's all. Probably would have been carved like a dragon or something. There's a prow in the museum, though not from this ship. They found it somewhere else, but this one's could have been similar. Come on, we'll go along and see it, and then think about getting some lunch."

Trina brightened at the thought of lunch, and hoped her father wouldn't get too carried away in the museum, or they wouldn't be out till supper time.

"What's the little pointy hill called, out on the Market Glass road?" Trina asked her father. She was sitting beside him as they drove home, following a dizzying series of small twisting roads which he insisted was a quicker way than going by the main road.

"There isn't one, that I can think of," he replied after a moment's thought. "We can get over to Market Glass from here and come home by that road, then you can point it out to me." Trina's heart sank at the thought of more twists and turns.

But though he slowed down when they came within sight of Old Newborough, and though Trina craned and peered from the car's open window, there was no sign of the little green hill.

"You can see it from that road," she told her father, pointing to the cobbled road as they drove through the Square.

"Not very likely," her father said. "That road must be pretty well parallel to the Market Glass road. If you can't see it from one, you won't see it from the other. Have a look at the map when we get home."

But when they got home there were other things to think about. Then in the evening her father was out again. Trina spread the map on the dining-table and sighed – half because of the map, which she couldn't make head or tail of, and half because her father never seemed to be there when she needed his help.

"Can we have the telly off?" she said crossly.

"I wanted to watch the news," her mother said. "Don't you?"

"No," Trina said flatly. She slapped down the map and stalked out of the room. The sound of the television followed her through to her bedroom; it seemed able to get through any wall, not so much loud as just penetrating. It drummed at her, even with the door shut. It was always talking about how many people were dead: five, twenty, fifty, two thousand. Trina decided she hated it. She lay down on the bed and covered her head with her pillow. A picture immediately came in front of her eyes – something she had seen in the museum, near the dragon-prow: it was a dark-brown thing, a mummified body sitting on a rough wooden block with its knees drawn up to its chin. The face was sunk out of sight as if it were gazing down at its hollowed-out body and wondering where its stomach had gone.

The next day she went to see Pats, but then decided she would go up to the Square first, just to look...

This time, she didn't hesitate at the entrance to the narrow street. She stepped out decidedly. She would get her bearings right, and then she would pinpoint where the place should be on the map. She would ask Pats' father what it was called. She would...

She stopped and stared. The hill was twice – three times – the size it had been the week before.

There was no doubt about it. It was the same hill; there were no others in the area with that definite, pyramid shape. It was green and grassy, with here and there the darker green of clumps of trees, and on the top a new, darker patch, as if the top was heathery ground. There was the road, there was the Cottage Wood; and there was the hill, exactly where it had been before, exactly the same hill. Except that it had grown...

"Pats," she said, a little later, "I've found a hill that's growing."

Pats stared hard at something just beyond

21

her left shoulder, rocking on his heels. "B–b–b–b–" he said against the back of his hand.

Trina wanted to share her discovery with someone, but she didn't get the chance just then to tell Pats' father.

She told her parents instead, and even managed to persuade them to walk over to the old Square with her, then up the little quiet street. The street became the stony track, and Trina stopped and pointed in triumph.

"That's Station Hill," her mother said.

"It's a good way of getting us out for a walk," her father smiled. "Growing hills indeed – I almost believed you! I certainly feel better for it, though."

"But you said there wasn't a hill on this side of the town," Trina protested.

"When did I say that?"

"Yesterday, in the car," said Trina. "We came back this way specially, and we slowed down so we could look properly, and—"

"Not me, darling," her father smiled. "I've always known about Station Hill."

"But it – the size…" Trina tailed off.

"Station Hill's always been that size, silly," her mother said. "Come on, let's turn back now, it's chilly."

"We'll walk to it in the summer, I promise," her father said.

Trina suddenly felt very tired; there was something wrong. She went straight to her room when they got home and lay down on the bed. Cat followed her in and sat crouched on the chest-of-drawers, regarding her silently from unwinking golden eyes.

It was at this time that she started having dreams. They were not ordinary dreams – they were linked together too sensibly for ordinary dreams. On the first night, there was just a kind of brown gloom that was full of voices. It was almost like being buried under the earth, except that she could breathe normally. A tunnel, perhaps. The voices were most unpleasant – they seemed to be gibbering nonsense, or making a noise like jeering laughter, or occasionally breaking into a high-pitched wail. There was also a constant whirring sound, as though someone had startled a flock of pigeons...

The next night, she dreamed of a quiet, sunny place of grass and trees with white blossom. She knew that this place was quite high up in the mountains, though she couldn't actually see any mountains. There were some small, rough ponies eating the short grass among the trees and, always just beyond, behind the ponies, some young people about her own age. She could never see their faces clearly. There were two boys and two girls, she thought.

In the other dreams, she kept seeing these same four friends. She knew they were the same four, though she could never get a proper look at them. Sometimes they would be riding the ponies, sometimes sitting around talking, on one occasion in a dark golden circle of candlelight. Once they seemed to be digging and weeding in a garden, laughing and carrying on as they did so. She began to long to be with them – there was something about their friendship that seemed so close, so easy and comfortable, so right, that she wanted to be part of it all. She would wake up from these dreams feeling lonely, feeling that all the other people she knew were somehow not the real friends she had always wanted.

On another occasion she had the dark dream again, but for a brief instant the tunnel, or whatever it was, split open, and she was looking up at mountains under a clear blue sky. So the two different parts of the dreams were tied together.

The dreams stopped coming so regularly after the first week, but every now and then she would find herself back in them. And almost before she noticed, she was withdrawing, finding it more and more difficult to keep interested in her friends at school because she kept on thinking about the four friends with their ponies and their mountains.

* * *

In the middle of that first week of dreams, something else happened. They were not good days: school during the daytime, evenings bickering with her mother, her father away, the hateful television pounding on and on. She was setting the table on Wednesday evening, when she heard her mother give a small gasp and stare at the television. Trina hadn't been listening, but she looked round all the same. The man on the television was talking about how difficult it was to get to some particular place because there were mountains and snow and no roads. Then there was a film taken from the air of some mountains, grey and white and mud-coloured, with dark patches of forest.

"These things always happen in threes," her mother said in a low, tense voice.

"What is it? What's wrong?" Trina asked. Panic was gathering inside her.

"A plane, didn't you hear? It's crashed there somewhere. About two hundred people dead, they think—"

Crash. The cutlery fell on the floor. Trina had clapped her hands over her ears. For a moment she gazed down at the scattered steel at her feet, then she ran from the room, her hands still covering her ears, kicked open the door to her own room, kicked it to again behind her and flung herself on the bed, burrowing her head under her pillow.

And exactly as it had happened before, the picture sprang to her mind of the old hollowed-out mummy in the museum, and a voice in her ears said, *Tell-evasion*.

She threw off the pillow. She could hear no words, just the rhythm of the newsman's voice: *Ba–ba bam bam bom, ba–bom bom–ba–ba...* She raised herself on her arm and looked up.

Cat was on the chest-of-drawers again, regarding her fixedly with his lampish eyes. Trina shook her head. Who had said that – *television* – with a strange accent? Why should she hear that?

She began to wonder what her mother had meant by saying these things came in threes. Had there been another crash recently, or was she thinking about the crash when Kitty had gone?

Cat got up, stretched himself, knocked over Trina's small mirror, and stood listening, as if to the continuing *ba–ba–bam bom* of the television voice. Then he poured himself off the chest-of-drawers, the golden-brown ridge on his back rippling, landed with a soft thump on the floor, and squeezed himself through the crack of the door.

"I wonder where Cat's got to," said Trina at breakfast time, a week later.

"Who?" said her father.

"Cat," said Trina.

"Who's Cat?" her mother asked.

"Cat!" Trina said impatiently. "What do you mean, who's Cat? Cat – our cat – Cat!"

"What is the matter with you, Trina?" her mother said. "First it was hills that weren't there before, then it was hills that were growing, and now it's cats. You're dreaming too much. I think you're having too much to do with that poor boy."

Her mother's pity for Pats always annoyed Trina. "Look," she said rudely, "whose dish do you think that is on the floor?" She stopped abruptly and shut her mouth with a soft gulp. The place where Cat's dish always sat was empty. There wasn't even a trace of the faint, discoloured ring it left on the floor. "What have you done with it?" she demanded accusingly.

Her father was looking at her intently, his eyes screwed up. "What's wrong, Trin?" he asked gently.

Trina got up from her chair. She scraped it back over the floor and backed away towards the door. She was appalled by the look of worry on both her parents' faces. "Nothing," she mumbled eventually, halfway to the door. "Nothing, I'm sorry."

Half an hour later, she was on the way to Station Hill. It was a grey, drab day but the air was soft – ideal for walking, neither too hot nor too cold.

She was not surprised to see that the hill had grown again. In fact it was no longer a hill, but a miniature mountain. The top reach of it had a grey, moorland look, and there was even a rocky cliff at the very top, but the lower slopes were covered with greenery.

The hard track became a rutted track, and then the rutted track became a narrow path. The path led her straight towards the little mountain before taking her over a stile and then losing itself in a grassy field. Trina continued in the same direction, though she felt a little cheated at no longer having a path to follow. Then she came to the river, and had to turn to go along its bank.

Now things became really difficult. The ground became a tangle of brambles, thorns, and thickets of young trees. Again and again Trina was forced out of the way she wanted to go, and completely lost sight of her goal.

She glimpsed a bank ahead, which looked vaguely familiar. She struggled on, scrambled up it, pushed her way through an old, baggy fence at the top –

And stood on the hard-packed gravel of the old railway course. She grunted, pushing the hair away from her damp forehead; if she had simply gone to the Cottage Wood and followed the old railway she could have had a straightforward journey. But then, she thought frowning, she had never seen her hill from the railway…

But what had happened to her hill? It wasn't that she couldn't see it now; indeed the whole trouble was that she couldn't see anything else! She was looking across the river to a full-sized mountain, with steep heathery slopes and long, dreary screes. She felt closed in, menaced by its great bulk.

Trina had thought she would climb Station Hill that day. Now she had second thoughts, and looked about her, trying to decide what to do.

There was a building ahead, indistinct against the thick-packed stems of the young trees. She went towards it hesitantly.

It was the remains of an old country railway station. The platform was a blue mist of speedwell flowers dotted with yellow dandelions. The station building was little more than a hut with brown planks along the front and boarded-up windows. It was very quiet, very desolate. The only sounds were the murmur of the river and the occasional peep of a bird amongst the trees.

There was a door to the station hut. Trina tried the handle, but it was locked. She sat down on the stones at the edge of the flower-grown platform, gazing for a while at the huge flank of the mountain.

A sound that seemed to start as a soft booming of wind, coming from nowhere in particular, grew gradually louder. Trina only half listened, realizing fairly quickly that it was the sound of a jet somewhere above. After a moment or two she thought, with a slight twinge of unease, that it wasn't fading away again as fast as she would have liked it to. It became an irritating rumbling grumble that seemed to be echoing backwards and forwards among the grey clouds, now louder, now quieter. Trina found that her heart had begun to beat quicker, and there was an unpleasant prickly feeling in her armpits. She frowned, and the thought of the plane-crash on the television came back to her.

She stirred to get to her feet, but then suddenly became quite still, frozen with shock. There was another sound. It came from up in the sky too – part of the aeroplane sound perhaps, but different, not the same as the to-and-fro rumbling. It was almost like a deep-throated shout, a huge sound though far away, up there in the clouds. A moment later a gust of wind set the leaves shivering on all the small trees round about. When it became still again, Trina could hear that the sound of the jet had changed; it was coming closer, very rapidly closer.

She looked up, but could see nothing but the grey sky. Louder, and there was another noise – a strange whine – mixed in with the jet-rumble. Trina's hands suddenly clutched at her throat, she collapsed on her side, rolled over onto the flowers and then leaped to her feet. The plane was diving towards her – she knew it even though she couldn't see it. The air was banging and roaring.

She must get under cover. Where could she go? She turned frantically, first towards the station hut, then to the thick-growing trees along the railway line. Where would be safe?

The din was incredible. She staggered towards the hut, but tripped over her own feet and came down on hands and knees before she could reach the door. The roaring was behind her now – low, no higher than the top of the mountain. There was a continuous high-pitched scream mixed with it, then a shrieking and grinding, then the sound became strangely muffled. Suddenly it faded, then died away, but smaller, confused sounds followed it – sudden dull bumps and strange creaks. There was something about the quietness that was even worse than the roaring and screaming. Trina crawled, endlessly, towards the door of the shed – she didn't know why, because she knew it was locked; there was no safety there. She had almost reached the doorstep when a tremendous *bang!* followed by a blast of air, sent her sprawling forwards against the wooden boards. Then everything went black.

3

TELL-EVASION

A dim *wa–wa–wa* sound was in her ears, and when her eyes flickered open there were grey-green spikes of grass in front of them. Blades of grass, Trina thought, a little tiredly and a little sadly – blades of grass, you can't do anything with blades of grass. She realized she must have fainted. She lifted her cheek from the stones it had been lying against, but the *wa–wa–wa*ing kept her from raising her head too much. She felt sick.

She was looking at two rounded brown things which she thought at first must be large toadstools. But there was something wrong with the shape. They didn't have stalks. There was something behind them – rows of little dark crescents. Where had she seen something like that before?

Bootlaces. She was looking at a pair of boots.

There was a stockinged leg in each of them. She scrambled suddenly back, swayed into a crouching position, and gaped up at the person who was standing in the doorway of the shed...

It was not a very alarming person. It was an old woman, not very tall, extremely thin, dressed in a simple shift of mud-coloured wool. On her feet was a pair of heavy, laced boots which looked much too big for her; her white hair hung out all over the place in wisps and wodges.

Trina glanced back over her shoulder. The mountain was still there, but there was no sign of anything wrong. Everything was quiet, quiet enough to hear the distant murmur of the river. No sign of the jet, no burning wreckage – nothing.

"Where did it go? What happened?" she exclaimed, as much to herself as to the stranger.

"Everything is correct," the old woman said. She had a dry, cracked, sweet sort of voice. The sound of it immediately made Trina feel calmer. "That was another's haunting," she went on. "But it is the opening of a door."

"Were you here all the time?" Trina said.

"Not when I was not here," the old woman answered. "But everything is in its place. You're not frightened, are you?"

Trina nodded. "I was, a bit. I feel better now. I did think I was alone, though."

"That is a difficult thing to think," the old

woman said, nodding her own head thought-fully. "But it is possible sometimes, it's true."

"I just meant—" Trina began, but the old woman went on, as if to herself:

"There are so many things, you see, that go into making a single person. Yes." And she nodded several times, as though she had just told herself something very important.

Trina began to think she must be a little dotty. "Do you live here?" she asked.

"Do I look as though I'm not alive?" the old woman asked in return.

Trina frowned. She got to her feet, a little unsteadily. "I mean, is this your home?" she said, gesturing towards the hut.

"Actually," the old woman confided, in a trembling, hesitant fashion, "I am a little out of place here – but not in an unbalancing way, if you see what I mean; I mean, it's necessary. I suppose you might say I am here in a tempo-rary capacity."

"Oh," said Trina.

"I'm more of a home myself, you see," the old woman said, nodding again. "That's why it's a little difficult for me. I am Mother Egg."

"Are you?" said Trina. She felt much better now, and she had a vague idea that the stranger was talking so oddly to her on purpose, as a way of making her forget the horror of the plane-crash – or whatever it had been. "I've never heard of Mother Egg, though I have heard of Mother Goose," she added.

Mother Egg bent towards Trina, until her dry old lips were very close to Trina's ear. "Without the Egg," she whispered, "there could be no Goose."

"That's true," Trina replied, drawing back a little.

"Now," Mother Egg said in a business-like way, briskly clasping her hands together. "You must listen." She put her head on one side in a bird-like fashion and said, "There are two things." Trina became very still; something made her feel she must attend. "Firstly, can you find your way back easily?"

"Home?" said Trina. "Yes, I think so."

"That I doubt," Mother Egg said drily; "but that's not what I meant. I meant, can you find your way back here?"

Trina found the old woman suddenly rather stern, and not at all dotty-seeming. She even began to feel a little scared of her. "I'm sorry," she said guiltily. "Yes, I think there's a quicker way if I just come along the old railway track."

"That is perfectly possible now," Mother Egg said agreeably. "The arrangements are all in place. The second thing is that you are suffering from tell-evasion."

"Television?" Trina said, remembering uneasily that she had recently heard that word pronounced the same strange way.

"Tell-evasion," Mother Egg said slowly, "is

a condition in which you are not listening to something you should be listening to."

"What?" said Trina.

Mother Egg turned and walked stiffly back to the door of the hut. For a moment Trina wondered if this would be the time to make her escape. Something stopped her. She had to follow the old woman. She caught up with her just as she went through the door.

"Look in there," Mother Egg said, pointing through into the darkness of the hut. "What do you see?"

"Cobwebs," Trina answered truthfully.

"That'll do," said Mother Egg. She sounded quite pleased, as though Trina had given the correct answer to a difficult question. "I too am a spinner, but nothing I make stays together for long. There are too many empty spaces. Another time," she went on, "I may show you the Scroll Cupboard. What's your name at the moment?"

"Trina – well, Katrina really – everyone just calls me Trina. But it's always been my name, you know – and I suppose it always will be."

"Really?" said Mother Egg, looking genuinely surprised. "I shall have to look that up. It's not impossible." She looked down at the palms of her hands – bony, paper-white hands – and murmured, "Nothing is impossible."

"I don't understand what's going on," Trina said.

Mother Egg looked sharply up at her. "Perhaps the end of the world," she said. "Perhaps something a little better." With that, she went inside and closed the door.

Although she was still quite mystified about the noise of the crashing aeroplane, and even more mystified by the strange old woman, Trina found she was feeling a lot better about things at home as she hurried back towards Newborough. Her shock over Cat and her parents apparently not remembering him had disappeared in the bigger shock of what had happened at the old station. She determined now to deal better with things. She mustn't cause arguments, or worries. She decided to tell Pats about her meeting with Mother Egg, but no one else. She would live two separate lives, one for herself and Pats, one for ordinary people. She would say nothing about the jet and the bang either, unless they had heard it too. She couldn't remember much about it now anyway – the thought of Mother Egg was far more real.

As she drew nearer to the outskirts of the town, she turned and looked back. The hill was there. It wasn't the towering mountain she had seen from the station, but it was decidedly bigger than when she had showed it to her parents.

"How high's Station Hill?" she asked her

parents next day, as casually as she could.

"What's that?" her father said. Trina noticed that he seemed to be paying her more attention than usual.

"The hill out on the Market Glass road," Trina said, carefully covering up any impatience in her voice.

"What, the Stack?" her mother said.

"I suppose so," Trina murmured. "I must have got the name wrong again…"

"I don't know," her father said. "It's not as high as it looks – six or seven hundred feet, maybe."

For the first time, the thought crossed Trina's mind that she might be going mad. Everything was confusion – the mountain; Cat; the crash. Yet from time to time, like a clear bell note, that strange name sounded in her ears: Mother Egg. It was a little like the dreams of the four friends, which still came now and again, though in very brief glimpses and snatches.

What was it Mother Egg had said she should be paying attention to? She was suffering from tell-evasion. It certainly wasn't news to her that she was suffering from television! She wondered if the thing she should be listening to was something on the television.

She wondered about the plane-crash on the news, but nothing more was being said about it, so she began to wonder if that had really happened. She didn't dare ask her mother if it

38

had. But there was a lot of uneasy talk about "unrest in the inner cities", and Trina's mother told her father more than once that she didn't want him to be in town if there was going to be rioting again. That, certainly, worried Trina, but she couldn't understand what good she could do by listening to the reports about it.

The more she worried about it, the more tense and anxious she became. For the whole week after her meeting with Mother Egg, it was as if there was something building up, building up in her, like water in a dam, ready to burst.

It finally burst on the Friday night in a terrible row with her mother.

The evening turned sour as soon as her father came home. He was back early, looking very glum. For about an hour he sat in the living-room, clutching a large glass of something. No one spoke until he had got to the end of the glass and then filled it up again. "There's no money for it," he said.

"What?" said Trina.

"You're joking," said her mother.

"Money for what?" Trina said.

"For his ship excavation," her mother said.

Her father took a long gulp of his drink and stared out of the window. "There was money for it," he said bitterly. "But the department's been asked to contribute to the new medieval village they're making at the museum. Once they've paid for the actors who'll stand about looking like medieval people in the medieval huts and paid for the machines that make medieval village smells, they'll have no money left for some serious research work on an ancient Burial Ship. I said we could reconstruct the ship – it's almost complete. They said that the medieval village would still be a better crowd-puller. In my day, children had to use their imaginations if they wondered what it was like to live in a medieval village."

"Children do love these things, Norman," Trina's mother said soothingly.

"Yes," he snorted, "and most of them are over forty."

He got up and started pacing round the room, picking up books and magazines and glancing at them and throwing them down again with a slap, rubbing at a small patch of grease on the windowpane, eventually striding out of the door, banging his shoulder against the doorpost.

Trina felt bewildered. Her father was always ranting and raving. ("It's because he cares," her mother had told her once, whatever that was supposed to mean.) But somehow, tonight, seeing him upset made her feel upset too.

The quarrel with her mother started so gradually that Trina didn't even notice it. First of all, she put the wrong supper-dishes on the table.

"I said dishes, not plates," her mother said. "It's stew and dumplings."

"Oh, what's the difference?" said Trina, who did not care for stew and dumplings.

"Don't be so stupid, Trina," her mother answered sharply. "You know very well what the difference is. Spoons too, it's a bit thin."

"Watered down, you mean," Trina muttered.

"What's that supposed to mean?" Her mother was glaring at her, holding the stew-pot in both hands with the oven-gloves.

Trina didn't answer. She went round the table, thumping dishes and cutlery down in the three places.

"Mat in the middle," her mother said. Trina thumped down the mat. Her mother thumped down the pot. One of the dishes jumped off the table and smashed on the floor.

"Now look what you've done!" her mother yelled. "Oh, you are so clumsy!"

Trina was already down on the floor, gathering up the pieces. Her eyes had filled with hot tears. "Yes," she blurted, "I suppose you think I am clumsy. It was you that did it, but it's still my fault. And I'm clumsy – I'm always clumsy, or stupid, or slow, or – or – anyway whatever it is, it's just what you hate and I'm not good enough for you and you wish it was me that had been killed and Kitty was just everything that was wonderful – she probably wasn't that wonderful anyway, but you like to think she was because it gives you an excuse for hating me and – "

She paused for breath, but at that moment her mother stopped her altogether. "Trina," she said, in a quiet, strained voice, "who is this Kitty?"

Trina stared at her. Was her mother playing games? Perhaps she was deliberately trying to drive her mad? She felt drained and tired. Doubt crept into her mind. The worried frown on her mother's face looked very genuine.

"Come on, darling, tell me," her mother said gently.

"You know," Trina said, with a half-sob in her voice. Her mother said nothing, went on looking at her. "My sister," Trina said. "Your favourite."

"Trina dear," her mother said, her voice so quiet it was almost a whisper, "you never had a sister. We used to call you Kitty sometimes when you were a baby, though I can't think how you could possibly know that – I'd forgotten it myself. But you're the only child we've ever had."

4

THE SCROLL CUPBOARD

She dreamed, strongly and vividly. She was walking along the cobbled street of an old village. She heard hens clucking and fussing from over a wall, and something that sounded like the rattle of a chain and the squeaking of wood from somewhere else. Then she was looking down a narrow path between bushes and the stone wall of a house, and sitting on a low bank of grass she saw the four friends. There were no ponies with them this time, only a small brown-and-white dog.

And this time she was able to recognize them. Not properly, because she couldn't see their faces from the front, but was looking at them from the side and behind. But she knew one of them was Kitty.

They were wearing the same rather worn, shabby kind of clothes Kitty and the boy had been wearing when she met them by the big waterfall; and she was certain that one of the boys was the same boy she had met that time with Kitty, though he seemed to be wearing a patch over one eye now. The other boy had very short, brown hair, almost like moleskin; and the other girl had dark hair and rosy cheeks.

The dog must have heard her, because it immediately turned its head, peering, with its ears pricked. She started down the path towards them, but almost immediately everything started trembling and the scene in front of her eyes broke up like a reflection in water, and in the darkness behind the breaking picture she knew there was the brown tunnel and the gibbering voices, and she forced herself awake.

An owl hooted. Where was she? Everything was dark, and after the owl had fallen silent there was no other sound. She sat up. She was in her own bed but had lost track of the time. The owl hooted again – in the trees over on the other side of the park it must be. She couldn't remember having gone to bed. She looked at the clock at her bedside – it said twelve but it had stopped.

She got up, felt her way to the door, eased it open. The hallway was dark, but there was a line of light under the living-room door. She tiptoed to it and listened.

The first thing she heard was her mother's

voice saying, "... must be, to be imagining things like that." They were speaking about her, then. Trina realized she must have been asleep for ages. She vaguely remembered now her mother helping her to bed, and giving her a pill with a glass of juice. Had they been talking about her ever since?

Her father said something which she couldn't make out, and then her mother said something about "the girl needs treatment". There was a long pause, and when her father spoke again Trina realized with a shock that he must have got up and walked over to the door. She meant to turn round there and then and run back to her room, but her father's words stopped her; froze her...

"She knows, Beth," he said; "knows what's happening. That's it."

There was an exclamation from her mother, and then her father went on in a firm, quiet, bleak voice. "She knows we're drifting apart – she may not *actually* know it, but she feels it. With other couples, they quarrel a lot and then one of them moves out, and that's that; or else they make things up properly. We don't do either of those things; we just carry on – we pretend everything's all right. She senses something's badly wrong, but she doesn't know what. She's probably terrified. She's imagining things. We're probably driving her crazy."

The handle of the door turned, and Trina

fled back to her room. She just managed to get behind her door before her father came out into the hallway, but she didn't dare risk the extra noise of getting back into bed. She crouched in the dark...

Her father was only going out to the bathroom, and after a moment he went back into the living-room and shut the door. Still Trina crouched where she was.

So that was it. They were driving her mad. They weren't meaning to. They were doing something terrible to her because they were doing something terrible to themselves. "Drifting apart" – that's what it was. It was the sort of thing that happened to other people's parents, she knew – she had never thought it could happen to hers. For a moment, Trina seemed to go outside herself; she seemed to be standing over by the window, looking at herself crouched by the door. And a pain, like a jagged white line, seemed to be splitting her head in half. Then she was back in her body again, and jerked herself upright. There must be something she could do! Something to save them, something to make them interested in each other again, something to make them care again. In a flash, all the past months, the past years, came back to her, and Trina saw the truth of what her father had been saying; something had been going wrong, something had been draining out of their lives all that time – ever since...

Trina shook her head. It was no use. She only had one set of memories, and she couldn't make herself believe it wasn't true. The truth was, everything had been going wrong since Kitty was lost. She could think of no way of getting that memory out of her mind. She had had a sister, a sister who looked very like herself. She could see her – she had just seen her in her dream; an older sister, with fair, curly hair and misty blue eyes. Kitty. Her mother must have been mistaken about calling her that as a baby. Adults did sometimes get confused about that sort of thing. Kitty was her sister, and Cat was their cat, and...

The owl hooted again, and a beam of silver light wandered into the far corner of the room. Trina went to the window and looked out. A calm, round moon had appeared behind the roof of their neighbour's house. The night no longer seemed dark, but the shadows of the trees across the park were deep and mysterious. Still staring out into the night, Trina slipped her nightdress off and reached for her clothes. Five minutes later she was climbing down from her windowsill onto the moist, soft soil of a flowerbed.

She had never been out alone at night, in the wide countryside. She flitted, soft as a moth, amongst the shadows of the bushes on the old railway track. She was glad at least she didn't have to struggle through the pathless thickets as she had that first time. The moon sailed across the sky and came to rest on the bulky shoulder of the mountain. It was so bright in her eyes and on the small, shimmering trees on either side of the track that the track itself was like a river of darkness that she was wading in, chest-deep, hoping there was nothing to trip on. Yet she felt no fear – at least not till she came in sight of the old station. She was too busy with thoughts of her parents, thoughts of herself going mad, thoughts of the four friends – thoughts of escape.

The deserted station with its tumbledown hut was bathed in silvery light. It looked peaceful and quiet, but something made Trina suddenly stop and look ahead in doubt. In a moment she realized why – there was the quiet, distant, high-up sound of a jet. There was no doubt of it. It sounded different, but it was a clear, cloudless night, so everything would sound different. There was an aeroplane, somewhere high up and far away, and it was coming closer.

Trina took a few steps towards the moonlit station. "No," she muttered, "please don't do it again – please don't."

The sound grew rapidly louder. Would she be able to get to the shed before it came? The distant cry, the whining and screaming, the shrieking and grinding – the explosion? She had to get there. But would the shed door be locked again? Would Mother Egg be there?

The leaves were shifting round her, and still the noise grew. She forced herself forward, and tottered into the sea of moonlight that filled the old station area. The door of the shed looked very firmly shut. Trina covered her ears and took a few more steps towards it.

And there was the cry. It sounded different this time – perhaps because there were no clouds – deeper, more menacing, more like a distant bellow than a shout. The note of the jet engine changed. Then the blast of wind came, and the trees bent under it and Trina was sent spinning round, staggering against the edge of the platform. The noise grew and grew and she found herself screaming through it, "No! No! Stop it! I can't stand it! Please! Help!"

And it stopped. It hadn't finished; it hadn't become as loud as it was going to. It wasn't the minute of quietness before the awful bang. It just stopped as though a radio had been switched off. Trina looked up. Mother Egg stood in the doorway of the shed with the moon transforming her tangled hair into a shining halo.

Trina scrambled onto the platform and went towards her. The old woman was smiling sweetly. Trina's throat felt tight. "What is it?" she whispered, gulping. "Why does it do that?"

"It is getting closer," Mother Egg said.

Trina was feeling shaky, but as before her fright was fading surprisingly quickly. She began to think again of the reason for her midnight visit.

"You've been listening, I see," Mother Egg remarked. "That's good. Now we can proceed."

Trina glanced around once more. Everything was peaceful, moonlit. "Please," she said in a small voice, "I don't know what to do – I'm so unhappy."

"Unhappy," Mother Egg repeated, as though she had never heard the word before. "My dear child, what do you want that you haven't got?"

Trina was finding it difficult to speak; "I want – I want – I want them to believe me – I want to know I'm not going mad," she blurted out. "I want Mum to like me. I want Kitty – I want Mum and Dad to stay together – I don't want Dad going away…" Tears sprang to her eyes.

Mother Egg laid a bony hand on her head. "I wish I could give you what you wanted," she murmured. "But there are more important things, you see. And there is nothing you can ever be sure about. Not in your life nor in anyone else's. You can't even be sure that the name you have today will be the same one you have tomorrow – or even that it's the same you that has it."

Trina looked up at the old woman, who was

gazing up at the moon. She felt a strange, silver quietness inside her, like moonlight, and she realized that she was waiting for something – something very important – to happen.

Mother Egg looked down at her. "If you're ready," she said, "I'll show you the Scroll Cupboard now, as I promised."

"All right," Trina said.

Mother Egg turned and went in through the dark doorway. Trina followed and the door immediately swung shut behind her. There came several minutes of blundering about in complete darkness, knocking into pieces of broken furniture, which seemed to be everywhere.

"Here are cobwebs," Mother Egg remarked unhelpfully, as Trina brushed the clingy strands away from her face for the fifth time.

"Don't you have any light in the Scroll Cupboard?" she asked.

"We aren't in the Scroll Cupboard," Mother Egg said. "There's plenty of light there – you just have to find it, that's all."

"That's the only light I can see," Trina said ruefully, looking at a thin blade of moonlight coming through a crack.

"Ah yes, of course," Mother Egg said. "I keep losing my bearings." She went over to the light and there was the creak of a door opening. Silver light streamed in, making the cobwebs glimmer like mist. "This way."

It was not moonlight. A dim, wide, empty hall – or perhaps it was a tunnel, for Trina could see no far end to it – stretched before her. Its low roof was slightly arched, pale in colour, and it seemed to be from here that the light was coming. The silvery light inside the Scroll Cupboard was dimmer and warmer than moonlight. That might have been because of the decorations all over the walls, which were of rather dull colours – cream, and brown, red and deep purple. Open-mouthed, Trina tiptoed over towards the part of the wall nearest her.

The decorations, which covered the walls from floor to ceiling, were all spirals of the same size: some tight-coiled, some looser, some no more than a short curl like a comma. Each one was framed in a brown square. There were thousands of them – millions… "Who painted them all?" Trina breathed.

"Tut, tut," came Mother Egg's voice from behind her. "You don't listen properly, and neither do you see properly." She reached over Trina, took hold of one of the spirals between finger and thumb – and drew it out of the wall. It was not a decoration at all, but a roll of something – no, of course, a scroll of something! Yet the Scroll Cupboard was not just the biggest cupboard Trina had seen, it was the biggest building of any kind; the arched tunnel stretched off into dimness in both directions.

Its vastness, and its silence, overwhelmed her.

Mother Egg unrolled the scroll and turned it towards her. Trina was a little disappointed to see that it contained no writing, but was all taken up with a complicated pattern of interlacing lines, boldly drawn in bright, lively colours.

The disappointment lasted only a moment. As her eye followed the swirls and curls, the breaks and bridges, the arcs and angles of the patterned scroll, she began to realize it was very beautiful, and more than that, it began to give her a strange, uneasy, excited feeling – a feeling that there was something about the scroll that she knew … that belonged to her…

"What is it?" she whispered.

"Names," Mother Egg responded matter-of-factly. "Just names."

"I only see patterns," said Trina.

"That's because your eyes aren't good enough," Mother Egg said. "They're used to those great gross letters you have to learn, and can't see anything finer. These are names, but they're written in very small letters, that's all."

Trina bent forward till her nose was almost touching the scroll. Screwing up her eyes in the dim light, she could just make out that the lines of the pattern were slightly rough at the edges, and the colours had not been put on with smooth, even brush-strokes but were made up of countless tiny dots. Yes, although she couldn't see it, she could believe that the lines were in fact twisting, swirling, criss-crossed, staggered lists of tiny names.

"Whose names?" she said.

"The names of all the creatures."

Trina's eyes wandered off down the endless walls of the tunnel again. She tried to calculate, then gave up. "I didn't think there would be so many kinds," she said.

"Kinds? Who said anything about kinds? I know nothing of kinds. Here are the names of *every creature*, their connections, their places, the patterns of which they are a part."

Trina was silent, letting Mother Egg's words sink in. But the thought was too enormous. She did not even ask Mother Egg the question that occurred to her – how many names altogether? – because she knew the answer would be quite meaningless, even if Mother Egg knew it.

"No scroll is complete," Mother Egg went on. "Each shows only a part of the great pattern. On this are written the names of two trees, and the names of the creatures which lived in them, and the names of the creatures which lived off them, and those which burrowed among their roots, and the names of the stones among which their roots grew, and the names of the mountains from which those stones came and the names of the rivers and ice-sheets which washed and ground them down; here are the names of the things which were made of the trees' timber, and the names of the small creatures which were burned when the branches were cut up for firewood, and the name of a girl who sleeps in the bed that was made from their wood..." She raised the scroll as she spoke until she was looking at the bottom of it. "Also, the names of the plants which died back as the trees grew and spread their roots... That's it, more or less. It's not a very big scroll."

"The girl in the bed –" said Trina – "what's her name? Can you tell me?" She already guessed.

Mother Egg started rolling the scroll up again, smiling knowingly at Trina as she did so. "We've had enough of scrolls," she said, "for they don't concern us. Now, I shall turn you into a cat."

"What, me?" said Trina, backing away a little. "A cat? Well, I don't – I mean – I didn't think..."

"Don't you want to be turned into a cat?" Mother Egg asked, in apparent surprise.

"No," said Trina. "I mean – well, I wouldn't mind – but only as long as I knew I'd be myself again when I wanted to be. I wouldn't want to be a cat for ever."

"No cat is for ever," said Mother Egg. "Cat is only Cat as long as the cat-form lasts. Just as Trina is only Trina as long as the Trina-form lasts. But have no fear; you will be able to come back when you wish."

"What kind of cat will I be like? Cat? He was a lovely cat."

"I will turn you into the only cat you can be," Mother Egg replied.

"When will you do it?" Trina asked.

"It's already done," said Mother Egg.

Trina looked down at herself. "I'm exactly the same as I was," she protested.

Mother Egg ignored her. "You will have to climb through the roof," she said. "There is a hole I shall have to lift you up to." She pushed the scroll back into its little frame on the wall and turned away down the long empty space of the Scroll Cupboard.

Together Trina and Mother Egg walked on between the endless scroll-lined walls of that mysterious place. The hall was quite empty and their footsteps made no echo on the sandy floor; and it suddenly seemed to Trina that she and Mother Egg were actually standing still, while the walls rolled past them like moving screens. Then Mother Egg stopped (or the walls did), and pointed up. "That's the place," she said.

"I'll never get through that," said Trina, looking at the small dark hole at the top of the pale arched ceiling above her. "And I don't think you could lift me up there anyway."

"Easy," Mother Egg said with a mischievous

cackle – and she grabbed Trina round the waist and tossed her into the air.

Trina was too surprised even to cry out; and then she was too taken up with making a grab at the dark hole which appeared in front of her face. She clutched, dug in her nails and hung on, waiting for her body to stop swinging…

But strangely enough, her body didn't swing much, and before she knew what was happening, she found her legs were creeping up under her and grabbing the edge of the hole on either side of her hands. Except that they weren't her legs and hands at all, but paws equipped with strong, sharp claws, covered with the silkiest, finest black fur. Scrambling through the hole was quite gloriously easy.

One moment she looked down, and saw a pale blob which she took to be Mother Egg's face, though it looked more like the milky moon – or perhaps a saucer of milk… The next moment she was climbing upwards from the hole.

5

CAT

Trina pulled herself up into darkness, but the darkness was moving. It was hard to say exactly how. It was something like swimming, and something like flying, though she herself was still. She knew at once what it was – the dark place of the gibbering voices and whirring wings. But was she really here now? She felt more here than the other times, and she liked it even less.

The feeling of movement stopped, and at the same time, for a brief instant, she had a glimpse of the world outside the tunnel: the blue sky, dotted now with white clouds, the mountains, and then the scene she had dreamed of earlier that same night: shadowed water, the smooth grey trunk of a tree, a stretch of sunny grass, and a grassy bank with people on it – three, she thought, not four… Then the dark place again.

The gibbering and wailing grew louder, louder. She wanted to cover her ears, but she couldn't find her hands. Then –

"Quiet," said an ordinary voice, a boy's voice, and the wailing died to a low, distant moaning.

The tunnel melted away. She was watching a boy walking into a dark, round room into which a beam of pale light fell from somewhere above.

There were stone walls, and a stone couch in the centre of the chamber, and a great shape of stone – a man sleeping – that lay on the couch; the shaft of light fell directly on a large-beaked bird perched on the chest of the stone man. Trina seemed to be looking up at all this from the floor.

For a moment the bird was grey stone also, then a ripple of black passed over it; the head and one wing moved; the beak opened in a gigantic yawn and snapped shut again. It was a crow. It shook itself, looked round, and its gleaming eye fixed on the boy.

"Herold?" the boy said.

The crow took a deep breath and its beak opened again as if the bird were about to let fly with a tremendous squawk. But the sound which came from it was the voice of a man, deep, quiet, and slow. It said one word: "Sparrow."

Yes! That was the name! The name of the

boy who had come with Kitty. Not Robin – Sparrow! But the boy was speaking...

"Is everything all right?" he said.

"Perfectly," the crow replied in the man's voice. "But there are things you should know. The time is very close."

"I haven't seen Puckel," the boy said.

"No," the man's voice replied. "But you have seen the men of the five villages setting off to find if there's a way out of the mountains."

"We thought that was a bit of a joke," the boy said.

"It will certainly lead nowhere, but it is a sign of how near the time has come. And now there is a breath of air in the Scroll Cupboard. Perhaps that will be the bridge end. I thought it might have been here, in the Vault of the Bear, but it wouldn't have been safe."

"Why not?"

"There are reasons. The dead and the living come too close here. Only the living can come to the Scroll Cupboard."

Trina's head was in a spin – the Scroll Cupboard... The bridge end...

"I don't understand about the bridge," said the boy. (You can say that again, thought Trina.)

"You will. Very soon. You will see Puckel, and he'll explain," answered the crow with the man's voice.

"Puckel explain? Everything just gets complicated when he explains. Then he disappears and you don't see him for years."

"Everything will become clear. Puckel has to watch and wait. He has done that for years – more years than you can imagine. The moment must be just right; it may not come again."

The boy sighed. "You're almost as bad as him. I don't understand anything. What should I do?"

"Where are your friends?"

"Just now? They're at the Hollywell – well, Kittel and Ormand and Lissie are. Kittel and I are staying with them for a week. Gogs is working at home. Bull was taken with the men from the five villages when they went off into the mountains. He's their big hero now, ever since the Troubles. They ask him things and he asks me and then goes and tells them what I've said. They'd never think of just asking me – they wouldn't trust me."

"You're too peculiar. Don't worry about it. Be glad of him. Go back to your friends at the Hollywell now. Don't delay – something is happening."

"Goodbye, Father."

"Goodbye for now, Sparrow. All will be well."

"Goodbye, Herold."

The next time the crow opened its beak it was to let out an ear-splitting squawk. Its wings flapped furiously, but the bird didn't leave its perch on the stone man's chest. As it settled itself again, the grey of stone crept back over its black plumage, and then the round room faded and the voices began again, and horrible echoing laughter mixed with the sound of wings.

"Quiet," said the boy called Sparrow. The laughing stopped.

Again there were glimpses of mountains, blue sky, a village turning on the ground below as though they were viewing it from the eye of a circling bird. Trina was still a cat, yet she was somehow here, with the boy...

"Here," said Sparrow. The whirring stopped.

There was a glimpse of huge holly trees, their glossy leaves shining in the sun like polished leather. Then there was the low bank of grass again, only now Trina seemed to be seeing it from lower down. There were grass stems, and daisies, right in front of her eyes. Gradually she realized that a strange shifting, dragging feeling was because she was in water. Not swimming – her belly rested on mud – but all her body except her head was under water. Two feet came into her line of vision, walking away from her, then two legs attached to the feet. The boy Sparrow was walking over to the bank where the other friends were: the boy with the mole-skin hair, the dark-haired girl, the dog and, lying now on her back with her arms behind her head – Kitty.

Except that the boy hadn't called her Kitty. He had mentioned someone called Kittel. It wasn't the same, but it was so close...

The small dog was sitting with one ear up and one ear down. Behind them were the bushes she had come down through, when she had dreamed before.

She heard the girl – the other girl, not Kitty – speak; but now something was happening, something was changing, fading. Yet the curious thing was that it seemed to Trina that it wasn't the four friends and their grassy bank that were fading, but herself – Trina. She was fading. She wasn't dreaming, she was the dream, and she was fading, while the life of the four friends went on; soon she wouldn't be there at all; none of her life would have existed... The only story was the story of the four friends and their mountains and their ponies and their old-fashioned village, where there was no electricity, and no booming television-voices, and no machines, and everything was quiet and green...

"Yes?" said the dark-haired girl, Lissie. She was looking straight at Sparrow.

"Yes what?" said Sparrow.

"What were you saying before you went behind that tree?"

Sparrow frowned. "Was I saying something?"

Kittel sat up, shaking grass and bits of twig from her pale curls. "You were moaning about how hard it is having magical powers," she said, with a yawn. "We were all feeling desperately sorry for you. And can't you take that patch off? You look like a pirate."

"It's sore just now," Sparrow mumbled. "My father – I had to go on the Secret Way... He had something important... It doesn't matter. Anyway – it's not magic powers... I don't mind them..."

He untied the strap that held the patch over his left eye and blinked a little. "It was simple when it was just magic powers," he said. "There's nothing wrong with them. I still like being able to fly, and shape-shift, and talk to the animals and that. Even the Secret Way is all right, though it's not as much fun – I mean, it's creepy...

"But that's not it. It's just that ever since they told me that all these things were *for* something ... I don't know... I just can't seem to enjoy them properly any more. Ever since they told me I had to start learning about the Secret Way, and we all started waiting because we knew Something was going to happen. It's all become different."

"It's been a long wait, anyhow," said Kittel. "A year and nine months. We could wait for ever."

"I used to just live here," said the boy with

the moleskin hair, Ormand. "Now I've been told I'm *supposed* to live here, and Lissie too, because we're the keepers of the well –" he waved his hand over towards the pool that lay under the shadow of five huge holly trees – "but how do you keep a well, for goodness' sake? The well's just there. It's like we're just waiting around too."

Everyone looked glum.

"My father said things have started to happen," Sparrow remarked thoughtfully.

"When?" Kittel asked.

"Just now. When I was away. It's what he said. He said we would see Puckel."

"Nice of you to tell us you were going."

"I didn't mean to. I was looking at the water and it just sort of – happened. It does sometimes. It was because my father wanted to speak to me."

There was a silence. Everyone felt a little awed about Sparrow's father. The people of the village had thought for years that he was dead, then Sparrow announced that he had found him and frequently went to speak with him. No one else ever saw him though.

"Anyway," Sparrow said, "he said that the men of the villages wouldn't find anything, but it was important they'd gone, or something."

"Huh," said Kittel. "It just means that next time the Council of the Five Villages meet, Plato Smithers will stand up and say there's no world beyond the mountains and I was just telling a pack of lies about it all – or else I'm nuts, which is what he's always thought anyway."

"Do any cats round here like swimming?" Lissie broke in.

Everyone looked at her.

"Course not—" Ormand began.

"Because," she went on, "that's a cat that's been having a swim in the Hollywell and it can't have fallen in."

They turned to the water. The dog's other ear went up. A small black shape was dragging itself on to land, though to be sure it was quick of Lissie to have realized it was a cat. It was more like a wet mop with a lump at one end. It shook itself and then sat down and started to lick. Kittel reached over and grabbed the dog, just in time.

"The poor thing!" said Lissie, and jumped to her feet to go over to the cat.

But the cat was having none of it. It was across the grass and off among the bushes behind them in an instant.

"Oh!" Kittel exclaimed, holding onto the dog, which was now struggling and squeaking.

Peering through the bushes towards the house, Sparrow and Ormand saw the cat pause, look back, then disappear off round the side of it.

"It's not one of ours, anyway," said Lissie.

66

"It looks as though it knows where it's going," Sparrow commented. Then – "What's wrong?" he said to Kittel. "You're as white as a sheet."

Kittel was still holding onto the dog. "It wasn't a cat," she said slowly. "There was something hiding in it."

"You mean it was someone in cat's shape?" said Sparrow. Kittel nodded. "Who? Puckel?"

Kittel shook her head. She looked less pale now, but she was frowning hard – as if she'd just seen a pig flying or water flowing uphill and was trying to work out if she could believe what she'd seen.

"Well, if it wasn't Puckel and it wasn't Sparrow, who was it?" said Ormand. "They're the only ones who can shape-shift."

"It wasn't who, it was what," Kittel answered in a low voice. "It was the dragon."

There was a stunned silence.

"It can't have been," Sparrow said at last.

"You only saw it for a second," Lissie reminded her.

"It was the dragon," Kittel repeated, letting go of the dog, which immediately went nosing off after the cat's trail among the bushes.

"The dragon's under the ground," said Ormand. "We saw it going there, and Puckel said that's where it belonged and that's where it'd stay."

"I often pass the dragon on the Secret Way,"

67

said Sparrow. "He's always asleep. He can't get out – and why would…" he tailed off.

"You don't have to believe me," Kittel said sulkily. "I'm just saying what I saw, that's all. It was a dragon in cat-shape."

"You're the only one who can see through shape-changes," Sparrow said doubtfully.

"Oh, so I'm just having you all on, am I?" Kittel flared at him.

"Follow the cat," said Ormand suddenly.

"Ever tried following a cat?" Sparrow said.

"Take Boffin's shape," Lissie suggested. "He'd follow it for a hundred miles."

Ormand whistled and shouted, and after a little the dog returned.

"Go on, don't hang around," Ormand told Sparrow.

"What'll I do if I catch it?" Sparrow said.

"Just go – see where it goes!" said three voices, all together.

Sparrow changed. He had been shape-changing now for over three years and could do it without thought or hesitation, as easily as diving into a pool of water. Sparrow's own shape was invisible now, but he was still there, his mind and his memory, except that his nose was down near the ground, his thoughts full of the scent of Strange Cat, his tail was waggling with excitement, his legs were tireless, his interest was endless – he was on the trail! He yapped once, twice, to the others, and was off.

6

THE GOATS

Sparrow paused, and took his own shape again. Boffin looked bewildered for a moment – animals usually did when he had taken their shape for a while – then looked up at Sparrow and flopped down onto the stony ground. He was exhausted.

Now it was Sparrow's turn to feel confused. He had been in the dog's shape for several hours, thinking dog-thoughts and seeing with dog-vision. He had lost his bearings. He and Boffin were far up into the mountains, above the line of the trees, among rough grass and bog and stretches of grey shale, and there was already a promise of dusk about the light. The sky had become overcast, and low clouds rolled over the stony mountain peaks that stretched in every direction.

This was the most mysterious cat he had ever

come across. He had seen no sign of it, but the trail was never in any doubt. This cat had done none of the usual things cats do – little detours to sniff or poke at something, little pauses to wash itself or stalk a bird or sit in the sun; this cat had gone straight as an arrow up out of the village of Villas, through the oak forests, up onto the moors, up into the mountains, due east all the time, without a hesitation.

It was no ordinary cat; but how could it be the dragon in cat-shape? What use would cat-shape be to the dragon? One use, possibly – to get away unseen from its great spiral den in the Star Wheel far off beneath the grass of the Valley of Murmuring Water. But if that was what the great beast was trying to do – and Sparrow didn't even know that it *could* do it – then why should it pop up right in front of Kittel, the only person who had the gift of seeing through shape-changes? The thing didn't make sense.

Ahead of them lay a rocky ridge. Sparrow rose into the air and hovered there effortlessly, while Boffin gazed up at him, panting, his head on one side, but without getting up. The ridge led onto a broad plateau of broken rock, and at the far end of it a mountain peak rose – a strange-looking mountain, steep-sided but flat on top, as though some tremendous knife had sliced off its true summit.

Sparrow knew only one mountain with that

distinctive shape – he had first come to it, flying, just after he had received his magic gifts from old Puckel. He had come to it on the day the dragon broke free, long before the dragon had been brought to its proper place in the Star Wheel, the day when Kittel had arrived, crashing to earth on that very mountain peak in a burning aeroplane – an aeroplane burning because the dragon had attacked it. He supposed the wreck of the aeroplane still lay there, but he never went to see it, and it was one place Kittel had never asked to be taken to. She was the only one who had survived that crash. The mountain-top was a graveyard for two hundred unknown people.

There was something moving down the dark flank of the mountain. Not the cat; it would be impossible to make a cat out at this distance. Nor a waterfall. It was more like a greyish-white worm. Vast, it would have to be – dragon-sized, though it was nothing like the green-and-gold dragon that Sparrow knew.

He returned to the ground. "Come on, Boffin, good boy, show me," he said. Boffin got up and immediately started following the trail again. Sparrow didn't take his shape now. He wouldn't lose sight of him here, and he could easily catch up with him flying. Boffin could look after the cat; he wanted to keep an eye on the thing on the mountain. They left the bog-land behind and climbed the ridge onto the stony plateau. The thing was still moving down the mountainside. It looked more than ever like a colossal grey-white worm.

On Sparrow's right hand the plateau suddenly became the edge of a cliff; a deep valley of stone opened up below, and grey water foamed and churned in its distant depths. The cat's path led along the edge of the cliff, but held on in the direction of the flattened peak. The worm, or whatever it was, had come down to the further side of the plateau, and began to head in their direction. Sparrow kept close to Boffin, ready to lift him out of danger if need be.

When at last he made out what it was, he scarcely felt any relief, though he was surprised. It was a column of goats. What they were doing up in these barren parts he could not think – there must be hundreds of them, thousands! Shaggy, dirty-white creatures, heads held low, clashing their great curving horns as they jostled in a tight crowd. They were coming straight towards them. Sparrow and Boffin stopped. The thin sweet billy-goat stench came to their nostrils. Sparrow snatched Boffin up and held him tightly under his arm, preparing to fly out of the goats' path.

But there was no need. At the last moment, just when they were within a stone's throw, the herd turned – and swerved off over the cliff. Sparrow's breath stopped in amazement as the silent, shaggy creatures, by tens and hundreds, flung themselves over the precipice. There was not a sound from them, not a bleat, not a whimper; no sound but the scuffling of hard-toed feet on the stony ground. Then even that noise stopped. Sparrow found he had closed his eyes. He opened them again. The goats were gone. He went to the edge of the cliff and looked over.

There was nothing to see. A sheer wall of rock fell to the river far below, but there was no pile of broken bodies. Not a single one. The goats had vanished without trace.

"I suppose you could call that tit for tat, really," a familiar voice said.

Sparrow almost lost his balance as he spun round to see Puckel standing behind him – Puckel, the same as ever, in his old tattered green-and-brown coat, with his nut-brown wrinkled face and the wild green eyes under their thatch of wild white hair. Puckel was never one for joyous greetings; when Sparrow met him, he always seemed to be continuing a conversation they had been having. "What's tit for tat?" Sparrow asked numbly.

"Not in any unfriendly way, of course," Puckel said. "She sends something this way, so I send something that way. Might as well make use of the channel while it's open."

"I don't understand what you mean," said Sparrow. It was not the first time in his life he had said that to Puckel! "What's happened to the goats?"

"What goats?" The old man looked surprised.

"There was a huge herd of goats," Sparrow exclaimed. "You must have seen them!"

"No, no goats," the old man said flatly. "You don't get goats up here and that's a fact. What would they eat?"

"But—"

"Dreams, thoughts, a few good songs, a few good stories," Puckel went on vaguely. "No goats. Come on." He turned and started off towards the plateau and the mountainside where the goats had come from and where Boffin had now gone, running swiftly along their brown-stained trail. Sparrow followed. By the time he had caught up with the strange old man he had recovered from his shock over the goats, and a quiet, pleasantly familiar feeling had come over him. He was so used to being baffled and bewildered by Puckel that their brief conversation felt like coming home after a long absence.

"Why's it tit for tat?" he asked as he came level. "Where's your stick?" he added, noticing for the first time that both the old man's hands were free. And, before Puckel could possibly have a chance to reply, a third question: "Where have you been all this time? I can never find you."

"You've forgotten where you are, young Sparrow," Puckel retorted. "All this creeping through holes and secret ways, you haven't been flying over the mountains as you once did—"

"It was you told me I had to learn the Secret Way!" Sparrow broke in.

"Not me," Puckel said.

"Well, your stick then."

"Not *my* stick," Puckel returned. "She does what she likes, old brittle-bones. I just try to keep it all together, which is no easy task as things are. Anyway, she sends this way, I send that – tit for tat. It's quite simple."

Sparrow felt light beginning to dawn. "Do you mean the cat?" he exclaimed. "Did she send it? Where from? And why was it a drag—"

"Best just come and see," Puckel replied, pointing towards the summit of the mountain.

"Can we fly there? It's beginning to get dark."

"I wondered when you'd think about that," Puckel said, a little huffily. "Don't know why I bothered giving you the gift of flight, the amount of use you make of it."

Sparrow knew better than to argue. He rose into the air, and then turned to see if Puckel was following. But somehow he was unable to control his turning, and the whole world seemed to turn once, twice, three times round him. And the next moment he was standing, with Puckel, on the flat top of the mountain.

He noticed the twisted black wreck of the aeroplane, like the skeleton of a giant animal, but there was something else which more immediately took his attention.

They were in a circle of buildings – rather tall, narrow buildings, all exactly alike, joined to each other by a low wall the height of Sparrow's waist. They seemed to be made of wood, but they were covered from top to foot in glorious patterns, carved and painted in riotous colours, blue and green and gold and pink and blood-red. Sparrow had never seen anything like it. The only parts undecorated were the low triangular doorways. The roofs were steep and tower-like, and covered in gilded tiles. The buildings were so bright they gave Sparrow the feeling that the place stood in bright sunlight instead of the gloom of evening.

"Like it?" Puckel said.

Sparrow nodded, turning slowly round and round. "What is it?" he said.

"As for what it is, you should know that," old Puckel replied. "What do I call it? I call it a medieval village!" He wheezed with silent laughter for a couple of moments, before going on. "We wanted them bright and cheerful-looking for our little guest, since she's used to bright things where she comes from."

Sparrow was only half listening. He counted

the buildings – five of them, spaced regularly round an open, circular area which took up nearly half the mountain-top. "It's the Enclosure, isn't it?" he said. "It was at the Hollywell before, but it's been moved here…"

"Something like that," Puckel replied.

"I've been trying to learn about the Secret Way. But there's so much I don't understand. I can never find the Enclosure, and… And I'm not even sure about the five places of power. I know about the Star Wheel and the Vault of the Bear of course; and I know where the Scroll Cupboard is, it's under that place they call the Echoing Hall, over near Springing Wood; and Mother Egg is where the dead lake is, but I've never seen it, and it sounds more like a person than a place to me. And the other place is King Puck, and that sounds like a person too, but I've no idea where that is – I've searched and searched and I've shouted at the Polymorphs to take me there, but they just laugh and howl and make me feel stupid for even asking."

"You haven't done too badly, on the whole," Puckel said soothingly. "You've found your way about, haven't you? The Polymorphs do what you tell them—"

"Apart from taking me to King Puck," Sparrow put in.

"They do what they can. There are some things they can't do, that's all. They're not going to let you know they can't do them.

That's why they laugh. They just want to put one over on you. It's a good sign. It means you've got them under control."

"Where is King Puck, then?" Sparrow demanded.

"Ah, well," said Puckel slyly, "that would be telling now, wouldn't it? Everything in good time, that's the best way. Anyway, as I was saying, this is our medieval village, and I hope you like it."

"It's very bright."

"And in the right place, which is much more important. Tell me, young Sparrow, how did you reach the Enclosure before?"

"It was through the Hollywell. Your stick told me that's where the centre most often was."

"And what did you do when you were there?" Puckel was speaking in a soft, sing-song voice, as though he were playing a kind of guessing game.

"Well – I – I found the Vault of the Bear, and I found the Star Wheel and – oh, I should be able to find King Puck and Mother Egg from here now, shouldn't I? If I just go into one of the houses…"

"Never mind about that now," Puckel snapped, suddenly changing back to his usual grouchy tone. "All in due course." He closed his eyes, and the dreamy voice returned. "And what else did you do?"

"I don't – oh, yes. There was a sort of opening in the bottom of the Hollywell, and I had to throw my stone through and I saw it falling through the sky and—"

"And what stone was that?"

"It was the one that had been the top of a mountain, and you shrank it by mistake when you shrank the dragon. You said it had to be put back so it could grow back into a mountain-top and..." Sparrow stopped. This was something he had never thought of before. What mountain had lost its summit? There was only one – only one flat-topped mountain, and that was this one...

But Puckel had shrunk the dragon, and the mountain-top, *after* the dragon attacked the aeroplane; *after* the aeroplane had crashed down into the snow on the top of this same flat-topped mountain...

"I thought—" Sparrow began, but Puckel interrupted him brusquely. "Time to go," he said.

Sparrow was at a loss. "But ... the mountain ... the dragon ... the cat ... Boffin..." he mumbled.

At that moment Boffin appeared out of the triangular entrance of one of the buildings. He was panting, rolling his eyes, wagging his tail.

"Saw him off, did you?" said Puckel. "That's a good boy. What a tracker!" Boffin ran to the old man and bounced up at his leg, trying to lick his hand.

"What about the cat?" said Sparrow.

"What cat?" said Puckel.

"The cat that crawled out of the Holly-well!" Sparrow exclaimed, exasperated.

Puckel shrugged. "Still crawling out, I suppose," he said. "Like us."

And Sparrow blinked, for they were. He and Puckel were ankle-deep in water, facing Kittel, Ormand and Lissie, who were standing staring at them, too amazed to do anything but gape.

7

INSTRUCTIONS

Puckel's appearance awed Sparrow's friends into silence. The old man waded to the shore and then walked over to the grassy bank, where he turned and immediately started speaking in solemn, impressive tones.

"The time has come," he said. "The time for which we have been waiting so long. I have gathered you here, and now I am calling on you to give your help."

There was silence. A pale ray of the setting sun escaped the grey clouds and turned the great holly trees round the pool to towers of shimmering gold. No bird sang.

"First, your task," Puckel went on. "You have a gift to carry – to carry to a place where it's needed. What is this gift? You are sitting on it; you are breathing it; you are feeding on it, living in it. This country of mountains, as you may now know, was built – its valleys, its forests, its waters, its villages – to hide and protect a great doorway, a doorway into the centre of the earth. That is the gift.

"The giants' doorways – those that can still be found – always needed to be hidden. This one especially needed protection because of the dragon which long ago escaped from it and was out there in the world, wreaking havoc and destruction. And because the dragon was not here, the Polymorphs also threatened destruction from within. Partly thanks to you, these dangers have now been overcome.

"But the effects of the dragon's time in the world are still as bad as ever. There is madness and destruction, there is dragon-poison in the very air. It is time now to build a bridge between here and there – a bridge so that the power of the Giants' Door may again cross over. This will bring healing, first of all, and then many other unexpected results beside.

"A start has already been made, of course. The dragon has been returned to his true place and the Polymorphs have been controlled. As a result of this, the roads between the villages have become safe. That is why people have started travelling freely between the villages. You could say, bridges have begun to be made. Lissie lives here now, not in the village where she was born. And people have heard young Kittel's story about a world beyond the mountains. The men of the five villages have got a search party together to try and find a way to it. They are trying to build a bridge, too."

"Bull's gone with them," Lissie put in. "He's the guide for the search party."

"Well, that'll set the cat among the pigeons," Puckel replied, with a chuckle. "Listen. There are many ways of building a bridge, but this bridge has to be made with the right direction. Otherwise it will be all wrong. You will understand this eventually. The search party are trying to cross from this side. It is important that they find nothing. There is a barrier. The bridge must be crossed from the other side. There is only one way to Kittel's place, and to find that way a bridge of dragon bones must be built to reach over the barrier."

"Dragon bones?" Sparrow and Kittel repeated together.

"Yes, dragon bones – bones from a dragon," Puckel snapped back at them. Speaking grandly always seemed to be too much of an effort for him, and now he sat down on the bank and rubbed his eyes as though he were tired.

"Where will we get dragon bones from?" said Sparrow. He was teetering on one foot, pouring water out of his boot.

"How does the dog find bones?" Puckel demanded, with a glance at Boffin.

"Dig for them?" said Ormand after a little pause.

"Now you're talking!" said Puckel. "There's a boy with some sense, for a change. Yes, you dig for them."

"But where?" Sparrow burst out, giving up trying to balance on one foot and squelching his sock down onto the grass. "The only buried dragon I know about isn't dead, and anyway you can't get to it because it's in the Star Wheel and you can't find it by digging, I know that."

"So?" said Puckel.

"So you need a dead dragon to find its bones, don't you?"

"What about the cat?" said Kittel.

Puckel sighed. "Questions, questions – you're always so full of questions." He stood up. "I haven't time for it. Ormand and Lissie must dig. Sparrow must take the bones and build the bridge. You must not do each other's jobs. Now it's up to you to get on with them. I wish you good luck, I wish you peaceful dreams, and I will give you a warning. This world where you live is built out of dreams. The world which the bridge will cross to is built out of dreams. The bridge is not built of dreams. The bridge is built of the bones of the creature which dreams the dreams. When the building of the bridge is complete, then comes the moment of danger – that is when you must understand the nature of dreaming so that the bridge can be crossed the right way. If it is crossed the wrong way, it will lead to the loss of the Giants' Door, and a catastrophe beyond anything I can tell you." He fell silent, gazing sadly over at the golden holly trees.

"What about me?" Kittel asked at last, in a very small voice.

Puckel turned sharply towards her. "What about you?" he snapped.

"What's my job?" she said.

"Same as it's always been," Puckel said. "To keep this turnip-head in order." He nodded over towards Sparrow, who was standing with his boot hanging from his teeth by the laces while he wrung the water out of his sock.

"Oh," said Kittel. She had no chance to say anything else, because just at that moment there came a hullabaloo of yapping and yowling from among the bushes, and a second later a black something shot out into the open, across the grass and, without a pause, into the water of the Hollywell, where it disappeared with scarcely a ripple. A second after that Boffin appeared in hot pursuit, skidded to a halt at the water's edge, and began whining and yapping and running up and down. Boffin didn't like water.

Ormand, Kittel and Lissie ran to the pool, with Sparrow hopping along on one foot behind them. The last of the sunlight left as they got to it and peered in. The water under the trees was dark, but not too dark to see. There was no sign of the cat.

Sparrow turned back to Puckel. "That was…" he began, then stopped. The grassy bank, and the lawn between it and the pool, were deserted. Puckel had disappeared.

Sparrow looked round in dismay. Eventually he shrugged. "Was it the dragon-cat?" he asked Kittel.

"I don't know," she replied.

They went on peering, stupidly, into the pool. After a while Ormand looked up at the darkening sky, and then down at the dark water. "There's just one thing funny about those reflections," he said. "The sky's grey – dark grey. I mean our sky is. But those clouds in the pool are white."

It was true. As they went on looking, it gradually became clear that the clouds in the pool were not reflections of the clouds in the sky above them. Quite apart from their colour, they were moving, as if in a wind. The four friends became quite silent, watching intently, for the clouds were changing. They were not now like clouds blowing across a sky, but seemed more like clouds rushing towards them. Every now and then one of them came straight for them, and then for a moment or two the pool was full of grey mist, which soon faded into cloud-whiteness again and then vanished, leaving the clear greeny-blue of an evening sky.

This was no reflection. It was as if they were

looking out of the window of something that was moving through the sky. And before long they realized that the darker thing just in front of their feet was ground – a flat plain, broken up into hundreds of small green and brown and yellow squares, small bumps here and there, irregular patches of dark green, strangely patterned brown things like uneven starfish... "Towns," Kittel whispered; "like when you see them from an aeroplane."

The ground tilted, and began to rush closer, bit by bit filling the whole surface of the pool. Bumps became hills, squares and patches became fields and woods. They were rushing with incredible speed towards a strange, mountain-less landscape; yet they were standing on the ground of their own country. Almost they stopped breathing, standing tensed, waiting...

A small, conical green hill came into view – not below them but ahead of them. The steep crown of it was in the centre of their vision, rushing towards them. "Go on, Sparrow," Kittel whispered, and gave him a nudge which made him step forward into the pool...

There was no splash. The hill rushed into their faces, disappeared. But so did Sparrow. And a second later the reflection in the pool grew completely dark, and then all that was to be seen of it was their own three white faces gazing in.

8

CRASH

Trina creaked open the door of the old railway shed. It was still night, but an eerie red light was flickering on the abandoned station. It seemed to be coming from the mountain looming in front of her – somewhere behind the summit, because she could see the black crown of the mountain standing out sharp against it.

Quickly she turned away, making her way softly along the old railway track back towards Newborough. At least it was still night and she might have a chance of getting home before her parents realized she had gone. She thought now how stupid she was to have run off like that; it wouldn't solve anything. She would have to stand her ground, she would have to trust her mother and father, she would have to trust that she wasn't going mad, and she would have to trust that everything would come right in the end. Even if it didn't, she would have to go on trusting – trusting something – trusting Mother Egg if there was nothing else to trust.

Why being turned into a cat for a short while should have made her feel so different she didn't know, but it had certainly helped in some way. She could not really doubt that she had been turned into a cat, although it was already beginning to seem distant and dreamlike. One of the things that made her feel it must be true was that her body felt so stiff and stumpy, and that she kept wanting to ripple her back, sink her hands into the ground in front of her, and saunter along on all fours with her hips and her belly swinging.

I suppose cats have no memories, she thought, disappointed because the only thing she could remember was curling up for a nap. When she woke up again, she had been sitting, in her own form, beside the door of the railway shed. Her mind felt strangely calm, although whenever she looked back to the eerie, flickering light she felt a tug of uneasiness. Surely it was a fire burning up there on the hilltop? It was hard to make out in the dim moonlight, but now that she was further away from it, the hill seemed to have come down in size again – it was no longer a mountain, but the size it had been when her father told her it was called the Stack.

She frowned at the moon. She had never

thought much about how the moon changed, but she was fairly sure it had been full, quite high in the sky on her left as she made her way to Mother Egg's hut. Now it was lower on the horizon on her right – and it was only a half moon.

Before she could think much about this, she was startled by a blue light flashing over across the fields – something moving on the Market Glass road probably, heading away from Newborough. Then there was a second blue light following it, and a third behind that. Police? Ambulance? What was going on? It crossed her mind it could have something to do with the fire on the Stack.

When at length she reached the Square, everything was in uproar. People were standing in the street, some of them in dressing-gowns and pyjamas, all talking excitedly. Every now and then the din of a siren would blare out, and a fire engine, or an ambulance, or a police car would turn into the Square and go speeding off up the Market Glass road. It was obvious something awful had happened, and Trina shrank against the walls of the buildings as she made her way down towards the Union Bridge.

By the time she reached the door of Pats' house she found she had all gone to jelly and she felt her knees were going to buckle. She stopped, banged her fist against the door, then turned the handle and staggered in, slamming the door behind her and leaning against it as she shook and shivered in the dark hallway.

A door opened and a beam of light shone into the hall. Pats' father was standing there. He had on a dressing-gown, but he was still wearing his trousers, and his pipe in his mouth was wreathing his head in bluish smoke. He had probably been working on one of his books before he went to bed.

"Trina!" he exclaimed. "Thank God you're safe! Come in, come on in, I'll ring your parents right away."

"No," Trina gasped. "You can't go up there – there's something wrong." Pats' father refused to have a telephone in the house, and when he needed to he used the public call-box in the Square. "I don't think they know I've gone," she added. "They were asleep when I left."

Pats' father looked at her searchingly. "Perhaps you're not so safe after all," he said softly. "I'll get you a cup of tea first. I'll be all right up in the Square, don't worry. There's been a big accident – a plane-crash, I think – but there's nothing to stop me using the call-box. Just come in here and sit down. I don't like to leave Pats alone, or I'd run you home straight away. There's still tea in the pot, fine and strong, just the very thing. Pats is asleep – just you come and sit down and I'll be back in a few moments.

91

Poor Trina, you're probably in shock. Did you know it's been a whole week since you disappeared? No, I see you didn't. The police have been looking for you up and down the country."

Trina gaped, and slumped into a chair. She hardly noticed when the mug was thrust into her hands, and it was only after she had been sipping at the hot, sweet liquid for a minute or two that she realized Pats' father had left the house and she was alone. But at that moment Pats appeared.

Pats was a strange sleeper. His nights were deep and long. His father said he doubted if anything would wake him – not even an earthquake. Yet here he was now, standing at the door in his pyjamas, looking at her, and showing no sign of sleep or bleariness. In fact he looked unusually alert...

In fact, Trina realized, with a shock that made her sit upright and slop some of the tea into her lap, there was something different about Pats, something completely new... Then it dawned on her – Pats was *looking at her*, looking directly into her eyes, not over her shoulder as he usually did. It flashed through her mind that he had lost his beautiful, faraway look and was much more like an ordinary boy now; and then Pats spoke.

"I know," he said simply, nodding as if to himself. "I know what's happening. But some things are a bit confusing. What's your name?"

"Trina," Trina whispered hoarsely.

"Trina. That's right," Pats said. "Of course."
Then, with a small frown, he announced, "You
need to dream. So do I. I'm going back to sleep
now." He turned and started out through the
door again.

"Wait!" Trina cried. "Pats, wait a minute –
I want to know…" She tailed off.

Pats turned again. "What did you call me?"
he said.

"Pats," Trina answered. "Isn't that your
name?"

"No, I don't think so," Pats said, frowning
even harder.

"Then what is it?"

"Spa… Spat…" Pats shook his head. "I can't
remember," he said. "It's something like that.
I've got to get to bed." He turned again and this
time was gone.

Trina's father arrived at the house, in his car, at
the same moment as Pats' father got back from
the Square, so Trina had no chance to tell him
the incredible news about Pats. In fact, for the
next fortnight, she had little chance to tell
anyone anything sensible.

Her whole world seemed to be turned upside
down, and the confusion in her own life that
night got strangely mixed up with the confusion and panic over the accident out at the

Stack. Her father drove her home, and one moment police cars and ambulances were racing past them with flashing lights and sirens whining; the next, the policemen and doctors and nurses seemed to have come crowding into her own room and questions, questions, questions kept coming at her from all directions. Where had she been? Who had taken her? Had she been hurt? What had she been given to eat? Had anyone given her pills of any kind? Injections? As the only things she could remember doing were going for a walk and being turned into a cat, Trina decided the only sensible thing she could do was to say nothing.

The next morning she was given an injection which made her feel very drowsy and faraway, and she was taken in an ambulance to the big city hospital and put in a bed by herself in a white room with a window that was just a little too high up to see anything out of. A young nurse who smiled a lot and an old nurse who never smiled kept coming in and out and feeling her forehead and taking her temperature and asking her if she was all right and if there was anything she wanted. Her mother and father were in and out as well, and occasionally another woman came in who looked at charts and asked the nurses things and never looked Trina in the eye. It was all extremely bewildering, and as days passed it soon became very boring. There was nothing to do except eat and sleep, and leaf listlessly through magazines and then eat and sleep again.

She dreamed a lot, but very little of what she wanted to dream. When had she last dreamed? Just before she woke up and wandered off into the night – or was it? Yes, that must have been it; the next time she had slept was when she was a cat. The dreams she had in the hospital were full of crashing aeroplanes and the barking of dogs, and Mother Egg walking slowly down endless corridors, and Pats continually appearing in doorways, and crowds of people milling about, and goats that kept turning up and wandering unconcernedly amongst the people.

If she tried to tell the nurses, or her mother, about this, they would just look sympathetic and stroke her head or plump up her pillows. The days of boredom lengthened, then shortened till she couldn't tell one from the next, and the only clear thought that formed in her mind was the thought that she would never go and visit Mother Egg again if it meant having to go through all this afterwards.

After a fortnight – though it seemed more like a year – Trina had a visit from Pats' father.

"Where's Pats?" Trina said. It was most unusual for Pats not to be wherever his father was.

"Wandering about in the grounds," he said with a shrug. "He wouldn't come in." Then: "I don't know what's happened," he said, "but he's suddenly started speaking. Not all the time – I mean, not every day – but, well, speaking perfectly; as though he's known how to all along. The little rascal must have been listening to everything we've been saying all these years. Do you know what he asked me? He asked me what the riddle of the Sphinx was. I vaguely remember talking about the riddle of the Sphinx – ages ago, months and months. He must have been listening…"

"I've heard of the Sphinx," Trina said. "It's that statue in the big concourse just down from the museum, isn't it?"

Pats' father laughed. "It was a lot worse than that in the original story," he said. "'A vast shape, with lion body and the head of a man, a gaze blank and pitiless as the sun…' You've heard of Oedipus? Well, the Sphinx asked Oedipus: 'What is the creature that goes upon four legs in the morning, and two legs at midday, and three legs in the evening?' And Oedipus had to answer it to save himself, because the Sphinx was going to kill him."

"What was the answer?" Trina asked, forgetting about Pats.

"Oedipus answered: 'A man, who in the morning of his life crawls on hands and knees, and at noon goes on his two legs, and when he is old hobbles along with a stick.' And the Sphinx let him go."

"That's clever," Trina said.

"You think so?" Pats' father said. He got up and went over to the window. He was just tall enough to be able to see out of it, and he was silent a while as he gazed at the sunny day. Trina watched him. Pats' father wasn't like hers. He spoke a lot less and he never got agitated. "You may be able to save your life by answering a riddle like that," he said, "but then it becomes a question of whether the life you save is worth living. A child could have answered the riddle, really – but Oedipus thought he'd done all right. But he hadn't. He'd treated the Sphinx as if it were stupid. His city was destroyed by a plague. I suppose your father would say he was exactly like a modern man."

Trina grinned. Her father was always saying that modern people were stupid. "What was the answer?" she asked.

"There wasn't one. The Sphinx was asking: 'What is this creature, a man?' And Oedipus just answered, 'A man.' No wonder he came to a bad end. He should have turned it round. I think he should have asked the Sphinx: 'Who are you asking?' That might have blown its circuits!"

He came back over to Trina. "I'll speak to your dad," he said. His voice sank to a whisper. "It's time we got you out of here. It's summertime out there. I'll work on him, don't worry – if I can get any sense out of him, that is. Since they told him there'll be no money for that ship project, he's taken it into his head to do it all himself – rented a shed just down the road from here; it's got a little room on the end of it where he eats and sleeps, and he's been carting the timbers over to it every night in a van, and numbering them all so he knows the proper order to put them back together. Always thought he was a little cracked, but this just about does it."

"He did tell me something about it," Trina said. "That's probably why they don't want me out of here. Dad's all taken up with that, and Mum's – well, she's got her work, and ... things..."

Pats' father said nothing; and Trina realized that she was just complaining because she was feeling sorry for herself. Of course they wanted her back home.

"Was it a plane-crash?" she said at last. She wasn't even sure if that had really happened or if it had all just been a confused dream-memory of that strange night.

He nodded. "A bomb, on the plane. The papers are still full of it. All those innocent people killed because somebody wanted to make a point." He turned as though he wanted to look out of the window again, but gazed at the wall instead, a dull, pained look on his face. "It's a terrible world," he said.

So it was no dream. And Pats talking wasn't a dream either.

After a short silence Pats' father said, "There's something else about this, though. In fact, everyone's completely baffled. The wreckage is still up on the Stack, most of it, and they've been up there sorting through it. They put the fire out a few hours after the thing happened, of course; but the strange thing is that every night it bursts into flames again, and they've got to put it out all over again. It doesn't look like ordinary fire to me, either. I've never been near it, of course, because they won't let anyone near, but you can see it from the town. It's a silvery sort of flame. And every night it starts again, and has done for the last thirteen nights."

As Trina fell asleep later on, she thought of the silver fire that would be flaming up again in the darkness on her mountain. And when she slept she dreamed at last as she wanted to dream.

She dreamed of the boy – Sparrow he was called, not Robin; but how did she know that? – in the dark, gibbering tunnel. The boy was certainly the same one she had seen sitting on the bank, the boy she remembered from the waterfall. He wasn't wearing the eye-patch now.

As before, there were occasional glimpses of the world outside the darkness; but during one of these glimpses she suddenly felt herself caught up – and she was outside the tunnel, up in the air, circling above the mountains, above a small, circular-shaped green valley far below.

She was dropping as she circled, spiralling down towards the little valley. Very soon she could make out details: a small dark line cutting it through the middle was probably a stream; an area with a different shade of green was a wood... There were marks in the green grass on one side of the stream, like circles – huge circles taking up the whole of one side of the valley. She spiralled down towards them. Soon she was skimming low over the grass – very low; grass kept appearing right in front of her eyes, and she had seen something like that before, but where? She seemed to be travelling round the outermost circle.

And then she was through the ground – underground; in the darkness again, going through the ground as if it were no solider than mist. She was slowing, coming to rest... Voices moaned and wailed. Wings whirred.

The boy was there, beside her. There was a rough earth doorway in front of them, and a dim-lit tunnel beyond – a real tunnel this, with walls and a roof. And on the floor there was a gigantic head – the head of a sleeping beast. The eyes were on a level with her own, but they were shut. Clouds of mist drifted around the head – or was it smoke? It seemed to have a smell a bit like smoke. Breathing it, she began to feel dizzy. And then it came into Trina's mind that the sleeping beast was dreaming.

Something was happening. Something that had happened before, only she had forgotten about it; this time she would remember. She was no longer dreaming – *she was being dreamed*. The great beast was dreaming, and she was part of its dream. Or … no; Trina was part of its dream – but now she didn't seem to be Trina any more. It was more that she herself was the dreaming beast. And now it – or she – was starting to dream about something else, and Trina was fading away, Trina was no longer there…

9

DRAGON BONES

"Copperhill again," Lissie sighed, as she always did when she came in sight of the village which had once been her home.

She, Kittel and Ormand were riding their ponies down the Old Road out of the mountains, and when they reached the place called the Cold Stone the valley opened out below them; and there, down amongst its green orchards and small, patchy fields, Copperhill nestled snugly in the warm sunshine under a haze of blue wood-smoke.

The Cold Stone was a tall standing stone, pierced through at the top, which stood beside the road. A little spring of clear water tumbled out into a trough at the foot of it, and here they stopped, as they always did, to let their ponies drink.

There were four ponies – small, fat, sturdy

beasts, slow, inclined to be bad-tempered, but much loved by the children of the mountain villages who, now that the Polymorphs had been controlled, made frequent long journeys on the old mountain highway. The fourth pony was Sparrow's, whose mother had insisted that he should have one and try a little to behave like the other young people, even though it was far easier and quicker for him to fly or go by the Secret Way.

It was three days now since Sparrow had disappeared into that other place they had glimpsed in the pool. The three friends were not greatly concerned about him – his life moved him on such strange paths anyway – but they did talk a lot about where he could be, and what he could be doing.

"Where was it? Was it your place?" Lissie and Ormand repeatedly asked Kittel, and Kittel could only shrug and say, "I don't know – it might have been."

"I didn't see any machines," Ormand said doubtfully.

"It's not just machines," Kittel said. "It's just ordinary country, really, just like here."

"I didn't see any mountains," Lissie said.

"There are mountains," Kittel said, "but not where I lived. Where I lived it was just houses and streets and shops and parks and gardens."

The last pony had barely raised its head,

snorted the water from its nostrils and shaken its mane, when Sparrow suddenly appeared out of the hole at the top of the Cold Stone and plopped down in a heap beside the trough. "Phew," he said.

His friends were by now quite used to him popping out of nowhere, and didn't waste time being amazed over this sudden appearance. "Well? What happened?" they all burst out together.

Sparrow scratched his head and grinned up at them. "There's not really anything to tell," he said.

"What!" Kittel exclaimed. "You've been gone three days, and there's nothing to tell. What happened? Where did you go? What did you do?"

Sparrow grimaced apologetically. "I don't really know," he said. "I think – I felt as though I was asleep and dreaming, really; that's what it was like."

"Well, what did you dream of?" said Kittel. "Was it the Modern World – I mean, my place? You must know."

"Probably," Sparrow said vaguely. "But it wasn't really like that. I saw your sister, though – I recognized her from that time before, by the waterfall."

"Trina? You saw her? Why didn't you say?"

"I just have. But it wasn't like that, really. It was all from funny angles, like in dreams…"

He fell silent.

"And didn't you see – anything? Anything strange? Cars, trains, just … real towns or something? When you landed on that hill, what did you see? Where did you go?"

"Oh, yes," Sparrow exclaimed. "I'd forgotten about that hill. Yes, I remember landing on it. And then I looked up, and I saw the mountains. Our mountains here, I mean. That's right. Only – I was looking at them from underneath."

"Underneath? Do you mean from the bottom of the mountains?"

"No – no, from underneath. I was underneath them. And then they were just clouds. But I'd made them become clouds. I didn't want anyone to see them. That was like in dreams, when you want something to be something else, and it is. You can do that, using the Secret Way and the Polymorphs, only I haven't learned how to yet. Puckel can do it." He frowned. "But that's all I remember," he finished.

"Great," Kittel tutted. After a short silence, she went on. "Well, meanwhile, we're making our weary way home, to pick up some picks and shovels and stuff and then we're going on to the Valley of Murmuring Water to dig for dragon bones. Do you want to come, or do you want to go on dreaming?"

"I don't think there'll be any dragon bones to find," Sparrow said.

"Well, there's only one way to find out," said Ormand, swinging himself up onto his pony.

"I can tell you," said Sparrow, "that the dragon's there now. I've just been to the Star Wheel. But he isn't dead. He's asleep, just the same as he always is. I don't believe he was ever in the shape of that cat, and if he isn't dead there's no point in digging for his bones."

No one could doubt what Sparrow said; but then, no one knew of any buried dragons except the one under the Valley of Murmuring Water.

From Copperhill, the Valley of Murmuring Water lay some two days' journey, by pony, eastward into the mountains. It was a deserted, peaceful, mountain-ringed circle of bright grass, with a small birch wood on one side of the stream that cut it in two, and very little else except a large clump of nettles that grew in the middle of the grass on the other side. The four friends knew that where the nettles grew there had once been a little ruined house. Sparrow and Kittel had lived there, during the time everyone now called the Troubles.

Three more days went by before they arrived in the Valley, as Sparrow's mother had insisted on spending a whole day baking so that they didn't go hungry. Murie was an easy-going person in most respects, but she had grown up in the days when it was unsafe for the village people to travel, and she couldn't quite get used to the way the young people would go off for days at a time. So she always found something to worry about, even if it was only that they wouldn't have enough food.

On the evening of the third day, they halted under the seven gnarled and ancient trees on the low hill at the western end of the little valley. In the silvery light of evening the sunken marks of the great underground spiral of the Star Wheel showed clearly in the grass of the valley floor. "This is the way the search party went," Sparrow remarked. "I wonder where they are now."

"Most likely they're on their way home by now," said Lissie, "because Plato Smithers is missing his parsnip wine."

"Bull will soon sort them out, if they start grumbling," Sparrow laughed. Although Bull was by far the youngest person in the search party, even the grown-ups in Copperhill sometimes found him rather alarming.

"Where do we start digging?" Ormand wanted to know. "Tail end or head end?"

"Tail end, thank you," said Lissie. "I don't want to meet a live dragon face to face."

"That would mean starting amongst the nettles," Sparrow said.

"And the foundations of the cottage," Kittel put in. "It would be hard work digging."

There was a silence. The smooth whisper of the stream and the tiny hiss of a breeze amongst the trees were the only sounds to be heard. There was no place as quiet as the Valley of Murmuring Water.

"We'll dig at the head end," Ormand said. "And hope it's dead."

After their supper they wrapped themselves in their blankets on the dry, mossy ground of the birch wood and slept, while their ponies wandered on the sweet grass on the other side of the stream. It was so quiet that they could hear the beasts munching, while stars peeped out and disappeared amongst the fragrant birch leaves above them.

The next day the digging started. It was overcast and chilly, which was good from Ormand and Lissie's point of view, but not so welcome to Sparrow and Kittel, who had been told not to dig.

It was Sparrow's job to catch some fish for their lunch, while Kittel gathered dry wood for their cooking fire. Sparrow took half the morning to catch only four trout. He fidgeted too much to be a good fisher. Kittel said he should take the shape of the fish and jump into the net and then change back into his own shape in time to scoop his catch out, but he refused. Kittel got her fire going and fuelled up and then took over the fishing; within half an hour she had caught another four. Sparrow went over and gave Lissie and Ormand advice about digging their hole until they told him to go away. He poked about the place where the cottage had stood until Kittel called over to him to pick some nettle-tops for their trout stew, and then pointed out to him that the ponies had strayed to the edge of the valley.

The afternoon went by slowly. The pile of earth beside Lissie and Ormand's hole grew bigger and bigger. There was no sign of them now unless you stood right on the edge of the hole and looked in.

There was some argument about whether Sparrow should help by moving the soil away from the hole, as it was slipping back in because it was in such a big pile. "After all," said Lissie, whose face was furnace-red and beaded all over with sweat, "Puckel only said you weren't to dig the hole; he didn't say anything about not moving earth." But Sparrow pointed out that to move the earth he would have to use a spade, and if you were using a spade you were digging. Kittel was never one to let Sparrow get away with anything, but she backed him up now. She had a clear – and unpleasant – memory of the sort of thing that could happen if you went against Puckel's instructions.

The soil was soft and crumbly, even at the depth Ormand and Lissie were digging, but there was no sign either of bones or of the underground passage of the Star Wheel. The last time an opening had been made in the Star

Wheel everything had been too hectic and nightmarish for any of them to notice how deep under the ground it was. That opening had disappeared now, and it was not even certain that it was possible to get to the Star Wheel by digging. But at least they knew that, if it were possible, they were digging in the right place.

The weather had brightened again during the morning of the second day, and it was about noon that Lissie broke through. There was no doubt about the moment it happened. One moment there was only the sunny quietness of the small valley; the next, there was a sound that made your hair stand on end – a sound both quiet and huge, like a sigh that lasted as long as it takes to count to ten quite slowly; a long, moaning sigh that was like a sigh out of the depths of the earth.

"You've gone all white," Kittel remarked.

"So have you," said Sparrow.

"We're through!" came Lissie's voice, as her head appeared over the top of the mound of earth.

Sparrow and Kittel jumped up from the cooking fire and hurried across to peer in. The pit tapered down to the small, cramped patch where Lissie and Ormand had been working, and where a small black hole was now visible just beside Ormand's foot. But whatever else might be in there, there was no coil of dragon smoke coming from the hole.

"Did that noise come from the hole?" Sparrow asked.

Lissie nodded. She looked white too.

Without another word, Sparrow slid down into the pit, bringing a small avalanche of loose earth with him. He squeezed past Ormand and struggled through the small opening, out of sight.

They almost expected another three-day disappearance, but it was only a few minutes before his head appeared again. He glanced up, looking pale and dirty. "You'll have to make the hole bigger," he said. "I think I might break this if I try to get it through."

"Out of the way, then," Ormand ordered, seizing his spade.

The hole grew bigger, and the patch of ground where Ormand was working grew smaller. At length Sparrow told him to stop and to get right out of the way. Ormand, Lissie and Kittel stood on top of the mound of earth and watched as Sparrow backed carefully out of the hole, holding onto something which none of them could make out. It looked most like a gigantic feather, bigger than Sparrow, and made of glass. "That's not a dragon bone, whatever it is," Kittel muttered.

Sparrow flew up out of the hole and landed on the grass some distance away from them. They ran over, but he shook his head warningly.

"Don't come too close," he said. "I think it's very delicate."

"What is it?" Ormand said.

"It's a dragon bone," Sparrow said solemnly, holding onto the great, feathery thing, which shifted slightly as the breeze caught it, glinting with rainbow colours.

"That?" said Kittel. "Don't be silly, how could it be?"

"There's a whole line of them, down there in the tunnel," Sparrow answered. "Lying on the floor, one behind the other. There's no sign of the dragon. It's not really like the Star Wheel – it's just a tunnel through the earth – but that's got to be what it is, it's the same place and shape and everything. I just don't understand it."

10

THE RAINBOW

Trina's father drove her home from hospital. Then, after hovering around the house for a couple of hours he muttered, "Well, I'd better be getting off," and disappeared without a word of explanation. Her mother, who had been given some time off her work, was doing everything she could to make things appear normal, and said nothing about Trina's disappearance or about her time in hospital. Also, she wouldn't speak about the crashed aeroplane bursting into flames every night, however much Trina questioned her. It was almost as though she connected it with Trina's disappearance.

And Pats, it seemed, had gone back to his old, unspeaking self. "It's a downright disgrace," Trina's mother said. "That boy could probably be quite normal if he just had some proper care. They should take him away from his father and send him to a special school."

"I like Pats the way he is," Trina murmured. Yet she couldn't forget the night he had talked; or what he had said – about dreaming.

Trina had to stay indoors for a week, her mother said. It was very galling, because she felt perfectly well, but her mother had got it into her head that she "needed to get her strength back". She felt like a caged animal. Her father came home on two occasions, but he spoke little and seemed ill at ease. Although he was there when Trina went to bed, he was gone in the mornings.

It wouldn't have been so bad if she could have gone on dreaming at night – even the confused dreams she had had in hospital would have been all right, though she really wanted to go back to the dream about the four friends. But there was nothing; she had stopped dreaming altogether. It nagged at her, because she kept feeling that there was one dream she had forgotten – an important one, probably the most important one of all. How did she know the boy was called Sparrow? That must have been the dream she had forgotten – but how could she get it back? She tried everything to make herself dream. She put books under her under-blanket to make the bed uncomfortable; she tried lying across the bed with her head and feet dangling over the sides; on one occasion she slipped two large spoonfuls of coffee into her bedtime cocoa, because she had once heard someone say that it gave you amazing technicolour dreams. She was almost sick at the taste of the disgusting brew, and the only result of her tortures was that she couldn't sleep for hours, and then when she did nod off she sank into a black, dreamless pit from which she didn't wake until eleven o'clock the next morning.

"What's Dad doing all the time?" she asked her mother.

"He's busy with that ship in the evenings," her mother said. She was chopping vegetables and did not look up. "He has to do it in his own time, you know, because the university won't pay him to do it."

"Will he come back here when he's finished it?"

"Well of c—" her mother began, then stopped. She also stopped chopping, and stared at the bright pieces of chopped vegetable on the wooden board in front of her. At last she looked up, looked Trina directly in the eye. Her expression was a strange mixture of her normal, organized, bossy-mother expression and another expression which Trina remembered from Max – just about all she could remember now of their dog – an expression of endless woe. "No," she said at last. "No, I don't think he'll be coming back here to stay."

Then she looked back down at her vegetables, and a moment later began chopping again.

"Will I be able to go and stay with him sometimes?" Trina asked, in a very small voice.

Her mother came over to her, and for the first time in she-couldn't-remember-how-long put her arms round her and held her close. "Of course you will," she said at last.

The week dragged to a close, and when her father appeared for a third time, at last Trina was allowed out. "Let's walk to the Stack," he said. "It's about time we saw what all the fuss is about. And then tomorrow we'll go up to the university and you can see my ship-building shed."

"I want Pats to come with us," Trina said firmly as they came down to the Union Bridge. She knew her mother would have objected if she had said it before they left the house.

Pats' father was only too happy to have his son go with them, especially as Pats seemed keen to be with Trina; and when Trina asked, he even said Pats could go with them the next day as well to stay the night at the shed where Trina's father was working on his Burial Ship. "Any day, he could start talking again," Pats' father said. "The more variety he gets, the more it's likely to happen."

The three of them left the Old Town square in bright sunshine, but by the time they had got halfway along the old railway track, thick dark clouds had come. At the same time it continued very warm, and soon numbers of flies were buzzing around them.

"Looks like thunder," Trina's father said. "We'll need somewhere to shelter."

Pats grunted cheerfully, though it was impossible to say why.

As they drew nearer to the Stack – Stack-size it seemed to be still, no mountain – Trina began to feel anxious. Would they hear the sound of the crashing plane again? Then a thought hit her. These things happen in threes. Twice she had heard it, and then there had been a real crash. That was three. There would be no more. Except – "What was that?" she said suddenly.

"Lightning, I think," her father replied. "Be quiet a moment." They waited, and he counted slowly, "One – two – three – four – five." A long, menacing roll of thunder crossed over the sky and back again. "About a mile away," he said. "I wonder if we should turn back."

A small, whimpering sound came from Pats. But he was gazing along their path ahead and not back to the black sky.

"There's a shed across from the Stack, beside the railway – someone at school said so," Trina lied in desperation. "We could shelter there."

Her father glanced back. "All right," he said. "We'll give it a chance."

They quickened their pace, every now and then glancing above their heads as the sky built up in great billows and towers. Intermittently the thunder grumbled, now and then shaking itself out of its grumble with a resounding crack, as if the very sky was starting to split open. On one occasion, Trina looked back just in time to see a jagged pink line running along the grey edge of one cloud with the menace of a pouncing cat.

"I think we'll make it," her father panted.

They did, but only just. At the very moment they climbed onto the flower-grown remains of the old station platform, a brilliant flash of light turned the colours and shadows of everything inside out, and at the same second a monstrous, slamming, tearing sound broke out above, below, and to all sides of them, as though giant hands were ripping up the earth like a carpet. A blast of wind followed the thunder and bent the trees over and sent Trina, her father and Pats hurtling forwards to the very door of the old shed. A moment later, without a drop to warn them, the rain was pouring down in torrents.

On finding the door locked, Trina's father did not pause. He stepped back and with a single kick sent it flying open, then bustled the two young people inside with the rain already dripping from their hair.

The noise was indescribable. It seemed the

flimsy tin roof of the shed could not possibly hold back the cataract from the sky, while windows and doors rattled with the almost continual battering of the thunder. The darkness in the shed was shattered again and again by the terrible flickering light from outside.

In all the excitement of beating the storm, Trina had clean forgotten to look at the Stack and see whether it was a mountain now or just a pyramid-shaped hill. Now, peering through the door from the depths of the shed, it was impossible to tell because of the curtains of rain and the sagging clouds.

Gradually the din lessened. She peered round the shed. All was empty, dust-covered, derelict. Slowly, she picked her way to an inside door. Was that the door to the Scroll Cupboard?

"Don't stand next to any windows," her father warned.

"I don't think there are any here," she said, going through the door. She was conscious of Pats behind her, peering into the gloom of the second room.

It was as dusty and empty as the first. Trina walked slowly round it, poking disconsolately at the walls, peering up at the cobwebby ceiling. There was nothing. If the Scroll Cupboard had really been here before it was certainly not here now. There was not so much as a hand-print in the dust. Dreams? She shrugged to herself.

A sudden light made her swing round. A shaft of silvery sunlight had shone through the door of the shed. Trina glanced at Pats, who had half turned too as she looked round. His face was only in silhouette, but somehow she could tell immediately that something had changed. His eyes, which slightly reflected the light, were seeing things properly again...

"Let's go out," she said. And Pats immediately went to the door between the two rooms and towards the outer door. Trina followed with her heart beating fast, certain that something was about to happen.

They went out into blinding sunlight, with every leaf and every bush sparkling. And then Trina found that she still couldn't answer the question about the Stack.

To be sure, there was a small, tree-covered hill just in front of them. But rising behind it there was a great mass of mountainside such as she had seen there before. Only now, that mountain was not the end of it; behind it, above it, one out-topping the other, other mountains rose, higher and higher towards the heights of the sky, while the grey of the lower ones merged into the pearl-colour of the middle ones, and those into the dazzling white of the highest.

Common sense told Trina they were not mountains at all, but only the clouds of the passing storm. And yet, and yet... She couldn't be sure. And as she stood there doubting, suddenly there was a rainbow.

It was not silently, serenely, there, in the way rainbows usually appear. They saw it leaping up and arching over from the high clouds like the path of a stone tossed down to them, like the trail of a diamond meteor. Like a shining mist amongst the trees it came to rest just inside the pink and white fence which had been put up all round the hill to warn people not to climb up.

Pats gazed at the towering column of the rainbow, and then exclaimed, in the sort of voice you use when you suddenly see the answer to a problem that's been nagging you for a week: "That's how it's done! As easy as that! Yes!" And with that he suddenly sprang into the air, clear off the old platform – and fell, with a sickening thud, on the stony track below.

"He's knocked himself out," Trina's father groaned. "Oh, Lord! What am I going to do?" They hurried down to Pats, who was lying without movement, and had turned a delicate shade of blue. Trina's father punched and pummelled him a bit, and at last Pats gasped, moved slightly, and then drew in a deep breath.

"Winded, I suppose," Trina's father murmured. "Am I imagining things, or did he speak back there?"

Trina nodded.

"We heard he'd been speaking a bit of course, then he stopped…"

Pats raised himself onto his elbow and reached for a stone lying on the track. He picked it up, turned it over and over in his hands, then brushed it gently backwards and forwards against his lips. His eyes were far-away.

"Well, he's back to his old self now, poor little chap," Trina's father said.

That night, all at once, Trina dreamed again.

That is, she supposed it was a dream, because her mother said nothing about it to her the next morning.

Somewhere in the darkness after midnight, she seemed to wake up – and with one idea in her mind. She had to watch television. Normally, she kept away from it. Now she knew she wouldn't get another wink of sleep unless she could watch it, just for a little.

She slipped out of bed and crept along the passageway to the living-room. She didn't put the light on for fear of alerting her mother, but fumbled about in the dark till she had found the plug, pushed it into the socket and switched on the set. Then she knelt in front of it and watched.

There was a black-and-white film on: two men making horrified faces while something black – presumably blood – trickled out of a wall. Trina was about to get up and switch channels when the picture faded and the screen went dark. She frowned and waited; this was peculiar. Perhaps the tuning was wrong...

And suddenly it was there – in full, living colour. It was the head of the sleeping beast in the tunnel, she knew that, but now it was head-on to her and somehow that made it look eerier. It was a golden head, very long, curving out at the foot of the screen into gracefully-flaring red nostrils. The top of the head was encrusted with green and golden scales, pointed and delicate as celandine-flowers. The huge, black-edged eyelids were closed below grooved bones that were like the start of horns. The mouth was out of sight. It was like a mask, utterly still. Was it sleeping?

It was dreaming. This had happened before. And when it had happened before she had slipped into forgetfulness, because she had been in the creature's dream – or she had been the creature dreaming of herself – and then it had started dreaming about something else. But that wasn't happening now. Something different was happening. What?

Something about the mask-like face moved. Trina watched intently. There it was again – it was an eyelid twitching. The creature was about to wake up. Again she found she couldn't move. If it wakes up and looks at me, she thought, I'm going to be sick.

And then the scream came. An ear-shattering scream that Trina didn't at first realize was herself. It seemed too loud for her to have made alone. Within seconds, it seemed, the light was on, her mother was there, there were exclamations and soft, soothing words, and then bed, and a hand on her forehead and the cool pillows against her cheek, and the black tide of sleep. But before the tide quite overtook her, the memory burned through her mind like a burning coal on a carpet – the beast had woken; its eyelids had opened; she had looked into the red depths of its pit-like eyes, and seen her own reflection.

That was not quite the end of it. She had hardly dropped into sleep when she found herself standing in a small green valley with high mountains rising all around. The sun was shining, a sweet breeze was blowing, and everything seemed easy and kindly. Then there came a shout from one of the mountains and Trina, looking up, saw a boy and girl flying through the air down towards her.

It was Kitty, and the boy Sparrow. He was wearing his black eye-patch again. It was only the boy flying, she thought, but he was carrying Kitty, holding onto her by the waist.

"Kitty!" she called. "Is that you? Are you all right?"

Kitty waved and smiled, but it was the boy

who answered. "She's fine," he called; "she's just fine. But what am I going to do with her? I can't put her down!"

And as Trina woke, she remembered; remembered the dream she had forgotten when she had woken up in the old railway shed – coming out of the water, the dash across the grass, the dog yapping at her heels, flight up the old village street, up the hillside, through the towering oak forests, the moors, up, up into the mountains. And then what? Goats... Something about goats... No, she didn't have the whole thing yet – but nearly, very nearly.

And with the memory of the dream there came a new thought – that when Pats had leaped off the railway platform, he had been trying to fly. No, not trying to fly – he had expected that he *would* fly.

11

BULL

"What am I going to do with it?" said Sparrow. "I can't stand here forever, and there's all the others to fetch."

"Make a pile of them?" suggested Ormand. "You'll have to have a pile of them before you can start building."

"But where's he going to build?" said Lissie.

"And how am I going to build?" said Sparrow. "I can't pile them up – I can't even put them down; they'd break to pieces."

"Well, you can't stand there like an idiot for the rest of your life," Kittel said, "so we're going to have to decide."

It was well on into the afternoon. The others had eaten the food Kittel and Sparrow had been preparing, but Sparrow had had nothing. He had hardly dared to move with the flimsy, feather-light bone of the dragon. Sitting down with it, or holding onto it with just one hand, seemed quite out of the question. They had talked through the whole mystery over and over again – whether the dragon was dead, whether it was the only dragon, what it was that Kittel had seen in the cat's shape. But always the conversation came back to the problem in the front of all of their minds: what were they going to do with this dragon bone, let alone possibly a hundred others?

Then the silence of the little valley was broken by a shout, and a swirl of birds flew up from the birch wood.

"Look!" Kittel exclaimed, pointing up towards the rocky ridge at the eastern end of the valley. "It's people – it's the search party. I'm sure that's Plato Smithers."

The others looked in silence for a moment. "What shall we do?" said Ormand.

There was a further shout. "I think they want us to go up to them," said Lissie.

"I'm off," said Sparrow. "I'm not going to hang around and let them see this thing." He set off, walking carefully up towards the clump of nettles, carrying the dragon bone slightly behind him as if dragging it through water.

"Where are you going?" Kittel said.

"To the Secret Way. I'll be back."

There was another shout. "They want us to bring a pony," Lissie announced.

"I don't know how you can make that out," Ormand grumbled as he went to fetch Sparrow's pony, which was the nearest. By the time he reached it and had coaxed it to him there was no sign of Sparrow or the dragon bone. "Come on," he said to the others. "We don't really want them coming down here and poking about yet."

It took them some while to get through the wood and up to the ridge. There seemed to be only two men there – one of them, Plato Smithers, easily recognizable by his huge size. They watched the three children and the pony struggling up towards them but showed no sign of wanting to come down. The pony wasn't able to get up the last, steep stretch and Ormand stayed behind with it as Kittel and Lissie panted on up the incline. Plato Smithers and the other man, whom they didn't know, started down towards them.

"What are you youngsters doing here, anyway?" Plato Smithers enquired, with some concern. Smithers, who was the largest and strongest man any of them knew, was always concerned about people. He was a sort of policeman in Copperhill, and not always very quick on the uptake.

"We just came out here – for a ramble," said Kittel, smiling winningly.

"We thought we might meet the search

party on their way back," put in Lissie.

"Did you now?" said Smithers with a guffaw. "Well, you're in luck, for we weren't going to be coming back this way, but there's been an accident."

"We're in luck too," remarked the other man, a small, foxy creature with red hair.

"We are, we are indeed, Bertie," Smithers agreed. "You couldn't have come for a – ramble – at a better time. Young Bull there, he's had a fall." He made a sign up towards the top of the ridge. "Broken his ankle, we think. He'll need to be got home. A pony'd be just the thing. We've had to carry him to here."

Bull was not the sort of boy who ever looked particularly pleased about anything. He certainly didn't look at all pleased now, though when he saw Kittel and Lissie his dark face broke into an expression of some relief, which immediately changed to one of pain because he had moved his leg. Plato Smithers heaved him up, as gently as he could, and carried him on his shoulders down to where Ormand was waiting with the pony.

"Well," Smithers said in a satisfied voice, when he had seen Bull safely settled, "we're not finished with our searching, so we'd best be getting back to the others. Young Bull will tell you what's been going on and you can take the message back to the villages. But it looks as though you were wrong about a way to another place beyond the mountains, missie." This was to Kittel.

"Couldn't you find it?" said Kittel.

"Well," said Smithers, removing his felt hat and scratching his head. "We found the edge, if you see what I mean."

Kittel shook her head.

"He means there isn't a way," the other man said drily. "There's just an edge, and then – nothing."

"Nothing?" Kittel echoed.

"Nothing," repeated the other man.

"Well," said Smithers, "there's clouds – blue sky, and great big clouds below you, when you look down. I don't really know where you got your story from, about another place, but I'm thinking you must have dreamed it. We're not giving up yet, though. What we're doing now is – " He broke off, peering down in some perplexity at the pile of bare earth on the valley floor. Then he scratched his head again. "Oh well," he finished, "best be getting back I suppose, eh, Bertie?"

Bertie said, "Don't hang around now," to the three friends, and then set off back towards the top of the ridge without another word. Plato Smithers repositioned his hat on his head and followed. Within five minutes they were out of sight.

Kittel stared after them, frowning hard.

"Didn't it even seem strange to them?" she said to Bull.

"What?" Bull said.

"That the world just – ends like that? Do they really think they're the only people living in the world – that there's nowhere else except the five villages?"

Bull shrugged. "Can we get off this slope?"

Until they got back down to the birch wood and more level ground, their attention was taken up with trying to keep the pony, and Bull, steady. Bull's damaged ankle had been well bound up, but whether his foot was in the stir-rup or out of it, each smallest jolt made him wince with pain. Once in the wood, things went a lot easier.

"What did he mean?" Kittel said. "What are they going to be doing now?"

Bull explained. "When we got here on the way out, there was an argument about which was the right way. I told them what you and Sparrow told me about that time when you tried to find the way back yourselves – how you'd followed the stream, then the long lake, then the river. But I told them it wasn't just as simple as that either – I was thinking of it all being a trick of the Polymorphs when you went before, though I didn't say that. I didn't think they'd be able to take that in.

"So anyway, I think they thought I just wasn't very sure. So some of them started saying that they should keep going due east – and that would mean climbing over from the long lake into the next valley. They reckoned that even if they couldn't find the old railway itself there'd be other ruined houses and stuff, like there was in this valley, and that would show them where the railway had been.

"Plato Smithers stuck by me, like he always does, and he said that he was going to go my way even if none of the others did. So they stopped arguing and said they'd just go where he went.

"But then the river disappeared into a marsh, and we couldn't follow it any more. So we just wandered on, until we came to an edge, like he said, and there was nothing. We had to decide if we would keep on going along the edge and see if we came to a way that went down – though you couldn't see anything below – or if we would come back to the long lake and do what the others had said and try and find the old railway line."

"So how did you break your ankle – did you try to go over the edge?" Ormand asked.

"Me? No fear!" said Bull. "I wasn't going near that edge. No, I just got caught in a rockfall two days ago. It was really stupid. It was that Bertie's fault. He was the one that wanted to go the other way in the first place; I didn't like him."

* * *

When they emerged from the wood there was no sign of Sparrow. Not at the pit, nor up at the clump of nettles. But Lissie peered into the hole and said she thought another of the dragon bones had gone. That sounded hopeful; perhaps Sparrow had discovered what to do with them. They told Bull everything that had happened, and then decided that the best thing now was for Kittel to set off with Bull, and make a good start before nightfall. Ormand and Lissie in the meanwhile would continue to dig and make the hole bigger for Sparrow to get in and out.

12

"AS EASY AS THAT!"

Sparrow had often tried to explain to Kittel and his other friends what it was like going on the Secret Way of the Mountains. But what was there to explain? To them, it simply seemed like a way of getting from one part of the mountains to another without spending any time doing it, the limit being that it only worked inside the vast, five-sided frame which Puckel called the Giants' Door. East of the Valley of Murmuring Water, or west of the Dead Lake, there was no going on it. Kittel now thought of Sparrow's sinister conveyors on the Secret Way, the Polymorphs, as some sort of bad-tempered taxi-drivers, though she had encountered them more than a year before and knew they were far worse than that.

It was different for Sparrow. He never called for the Polymorphs to come and take him anywhere, and he never actually saw them. He could make them appear before his darkened left eye, though this was something he hardly ever did. He remembered well enough the horror of the sight of them – their grey, distant faces, their humped bodies, winged and armless, Bur with his two one-eyed heads… He had enough to remind him of what they were like when he travelled on the Secret Way and heard their gibbering voices and wailing laughter.

He didn't like the Secret Way, and used it mainly because Puckel had told him to. Entering it was for him a bit like having to swim through a pot of bubbling liquid. The bubbling was the voices of the Polymorphs, and the thoughts that kept bubbling up in his mind. You had to keep control of them, or they would take control of you; you had simply to concentrate all your attention on the other side of the bubbling pot – the place where you wanted to be; and when you did that, the place where you were suddenly fell away like mist and shadows; there would be a darkness, as though you were under the earth but the earth itself were misty and unreal; there were strange, twisting glimpses of the ordinary world, and then the place where you wanted to be took shape around you, grew solid, and you were back in the world of everyday.

So it was that the clump of nettles, the Valley of Murmuring Water and the mountains all around melted away, and the smooth grey-green pillars of the five holly trees took shape out of the darkness. Sparrow stood beside the Hollywell holding the great, delicate dragon bone under the spiked shadows of the trees, and wondered what to do. Was the bridge to be built from here? He looked into the pool through which he had gone into that other place – Kittel's place. He saw only water, and the swift shadow of a trout in its dark brown depths.

Then without warning the darkness rose up round him out of the pool, and changed to light, and a gust of fresh wind lifted the feathery bone and almost pulled it out of his hand. He looked around him. He was on the flat-topped mountain with the wreck of the burned aeroplane lying within view. He was standing in the enclosure surrounded by the five bright-painted buildings which Puckel had called his medieval village.

"Puckel?" he called. "Are you there?"

There was no sound except the sharp-sifting wind. But Sparrow knew that if you found yourself in the Enclosure it meant that you were supposed to go into one of the five places of power that were hidden in the five angles of the Giants' Door. But which was which? And which did he want, anyway?

The Secret Way led past the places of power, but only by the Enclosure could you enter them for the first time. He had once been in the Star Wheel, before the dragon was returned to it, and had several times been in the Vault of the Bear to speak with his father. He knew where the companion-places of these two were – Mother Egg opposite the Star Wheel and the Scroll Cupboard opposite the Vault of the Bear; he knew that somewhere between the Star Wheel and Mother Egg was King Puck, though he had never found it; but that was all he knew.

Now he stood on the mountain-top and felt sure only that it was not the Vault of the Bear or the Star Wheel he was to go to. And what had his father said? That there was a breath of air in the Scroll Cupboard – yes! And that was where his father believed the bridge was to be built from. He went towards the nearest of the low, triangle-shaped entrances, turned to go through it, stooping, backwards, so as not to risk damage to his strange burden.

Immediately, a dim, silvery light was all around him, and he found himself coming through a doorway into a place which he did not know.

It was utterly still. He tiptoed along beside an endless wall, gazing in wonder at the thousands upon thousands of little scroll-spirals which covered it. He was in no doubt that this was the Scroll Cupboard. Now that he was out of the sunlight in that dim place the dragon bone no longer flashed with rainbow lights but glowed like mother-of-pearl.

After a while, he realized he had been hearing a scuffling, scurrying sound without properly noticing it. He stopped, holding his breath. The sound came nearer, but it wasn't until the very last moment that he saw the movement at his feet. There was a small, jagged creature with four legs on each side of its reddish-brown body and an unpleasant-shaped tail that curved up over its back into a deadly-looking, pointed end. Sparrow had never seen a scorpion before, but he had heard descriptions of them and he stepped back hastily.

"If you go on gawping like that, mud-head, a bird's going to come and make a nest in your mouth," came a dry, rasping, very familiar voice. Sparrow shut his mouth immediately.

"I didn't know you turned into a scorpion as well," he said, as soon as he realized that the voice, which was the voice of Puckel's stick, was coming from the little creature at his feet.

"Don't be a fool," the scorpion returned without ceremony. "If you're here to dump that thing, then dump it and go and get on. You're not on a sight-seeing holiday."

Sparrow could never quite get used to the stick's rudeness, especially since he knew there was a connection between it and the old teacher they had had at the village school in Copperhill, in the days before Kittel came – gentle, mild, dottled old Ms Minn. He wasn't quite sure what the connection was; he had seen the stick turning into a snake, and a bowl of water, and a rainstorm, and a waterspout, but never – exactly – into the old teacher herself. Yet he was almost certain that they were one and the same. At any rate he knew better than to argue. "I'm afraid it might break if I put it down," he said.

"Don't be ridiculous," the scorpion snapped, rattling its tail. "You're just making excuses for being so slow. Why, a tortoise with a lead shell could do the job quicker than you're doing it. Just drop it there. Let go."

Sparrow hastily did as he was told. His arms were stiff from having held them in the same position for so long.

The bone of the dragon remained exactly where it was. It didn't drop; it simply floated, without movement.

"Well, go on, go on," came the scorpion's exasperated voice. "Or do I need to give you a prick in the heel?" It raised its tail menacingly.

"No," said Sparrow, and fled back the way he had come.

The bubbling of thoughts through his mind, which was the voices of the Polymorphs, was all mockery and derision. The Polymorphs seemed to think it a very funny idea that he was slower than a tortoise with a lead shell. Sparrow's mind was full of pictures of giant, gasping tortoises scrambling up endless slopes or labouring across endless stretches of dry, cracked mud. He endured it, and was soon standing among the nettles again in the Valley of Murmuring Water. There had been no glimpse either of the Enclosure or of the Hollywell. This didn't surprise him, and he was fairly sure that there would be no difficulty in getting back to the Scroll Cupboard with the next dragon bone.

He picked his way among the stones of the ruined cottage. There was no sign of any of the others in the valley, but he was more concerned about not getting into more trouble with the scorpion. He flew down into the pit, wriggled through the hole Ormand had made, scrambled along the small earth passage and carefully took hold of the second bone. This time he flew from the pit straight to the patch of nettles. The Polymorphs started up a mock-enraged howling like distant wolves as soon as he entered the Secret Way again, but he ignored it. And as he had expected, the Way now led directly to the doorway of the Scroll Cupboard. He had made a little bridge of his own!

There was no sign of the scorpion as he skimmed lightly down the endless tunnel of the Scroll Cupboard. In the silence of the place he could hear the great dragon bone humming softly as he dragged it through the air behind him. He came to the place where the first bone still floated, motionless, exactly as he had left it. He let go of the one he was carrying, and it hung floating beside the first.

Sparrow looked at the two great, feathery things and wondered about them. Even if they could be left floating in the air, would they make a bridge? Perhaps they would be more like stepping-stones – but from where, and to where? And who would walk on them?

Gently, he gave the second bone a push with his finger. It was an extremely light push; he simply wanted to see if it was fixed there in the air. The bone moved, swinging softly round towards its companion. They'll collide! Sparrow thought, frantically reaching out to stop the two bones from knocking together.

A flash, like a rod of horizontal lightning, ran through the Scroll Cupboard. Blinded for a moment, Sparrow staggered back. When he could see again, there were the two dragon bones floating end to end, joined together by what looked like a small blue knot.

He stared at the two bones. There was something different about them – they hadn't exactly changed, but there was something about them which looked less fragile. Gently, he put out his hand again and touched one. The feathery end did not move; it felt hard, strong as steel. Amazement gave way to delight. "So that's how it's done!" he breathed. "As easy as that! Yes!" And he leaped into the air again, almost knocking his head against the arched roof of the Scroll Cupboard, and skimmed off back to the doorway.

Returning to the Valley of Murmuring Water, he saw Ormand and Lissie, but no sign of Kittel. The sun seemed to have disappeared behind the mountains. He wondered how long he had been away. There was no telling with the Secret Way – going from one place to another seemed to take no time at all, but in the Enclosure or the Scroll Cupboard any amount of time might have passed.

It turned out he had been gone about an hour. Bull had been collected and had set off with Kittel for Copperhill almost straight away.

"I've a better idea," Sparrow said as soon as he heard what had happened. "I'll go after them just now and fly home with Bull, then Kittel can come back here."

"I don't think you should," said Lissie firmly.

"Why?" asked Sparrow, who had already forgotten what the scorpion had said.

"Because you're supposed to be making the bridge, and we're supposed to be digging for the bones, that's why," Lissie replied. "Kittel didn't have a job like that to do, and she'd just have to wait around for us anyway."

"It could take a long time to get all those bone things out," Ormand put in. "And we don't know when the search party will be coming back."

Sparrow hesitated. "Bull needs help," he said at last. "It'll be two days before he gets home if he goes with Kittel. But I could get him home tonight. I'll be back. You start digging again; it'd be a lot easier if the opening was made bigger. I'll be able to get more of the bones before it's dark."

"You'll be sorry," said Lissie. "You should do what Puckel said. We'll probably all be sorry." She stalked off back to the pit, followed by Ormand. Sparrow watched them slipping out of sight down the pile of soil. Then with a shrug he leaped into the air and flew off.

He flew low through the valleys. There was no path to follow, but he knew the way well, as did Kittel and Bull. There was only one way to go, so there was no risk of missing them.

"They must have been going at an amazing speed," he muttered to himself as quarter of an hour passed with no sign of them. Somehow, he felt uneasy.

A quarter of an hour after this, he could not fool himself any more. He had circled and searched, flown high to survey the land beneath, dropped to the ground to try and find tracks. But amongst rocks, bushes, moss, pools and heather, nothing moved. Kittel and Bull had disappeared.

It was going to be dark before long. Sparrow had a sudden pang of conscience. Lissie had been right. He was going against what both Puckel and the scorpion had said. The only time he had disobeyed Puckel before it had nearly led to disaster. A cold sweat broke out on his forehead and in his armpits; a sweat of fear.

As swiftly as he could, he made his way back to the Valley of Murmuring Water. The sky had become overcast again, and low clouds were blotting out all but the feet of the mountains, bringing on the evening more quickly. He landed beside Lissie and Ormand, who were sitting on top of the pile of earth looking grey and disconsolate.

"You see?" said Lissie as soon as he landed. "That's what happens when you don't do what you're told. It's not our fault."

"What isn't?" said Sparrow, in fright. "What's happened? What's wrong?"

"We tried to move the next dragon bone," Ormand explained. "We were afraid the earth would fall on it and damage it."

"What happened?"

"Well, we broke it, didn't we?" said Lissie sulkily. "It wasn't our fault."

Sparrow thought about this for a moment. "It doesn't seem too bad to me," he said at length. "There's probably far more there than I need, anyway." He wasn't quite sure if he believed that himself, but it seemed too early to worry about it now. "Come on," he said,

"I'm going to get the next one. Stand by; I shouldn't be too long."

Lissie and Ormand remained where they were as Sparrow eased the fourth bone over the third one, which lay shattered in a thousand pieces at the mouth of the small tunnel.

Ten times more he repeated his journey between the Star Wheel and the Scroll Cupboard, before it got too dark to see in the tunnel, and Lissie and Ormand went off to light the cooking-fire. Twelve dragon bones now floated, knotted end to end, glowing in the dim light of the Scroll Cupboard. It had not exactly been hard work for Sparrow, but by the time they had finished their supper by the light of their camp-fire, he felt tired beyond thinking. Even before Ormand and Lissie, exhausted as they were, had started to yawn, almost before he had had time to lie down, he was in deep sleep.

13

IN THE CITY

"What a day!" Trina's father gasped, wiping his forehead with his handkerchief. The city streets had been stiflingly hot between the thunderstorms, and now, as evening came on, it was only a little cooler. The breeze off the sea would heave restlessly and then be still. The grey clouds which covered the sky seemed to weigh down on them, suffocating, as if they wanted to crush the tall buildings back into the ground. Worse than that, there was another feeling in the air, connected with the heavy clouds but not the same – an unpleasant, waiting feeling; as though something were about to happen...

The really strange thing in all this was Pats. He remained calm and good-humoured the whole day, despite the thunderstorms, and despite the crowds of people out on the streets in the sunshine between the storms. That was not what they had expected. Normally any kind of excitement made him nervous. Certainly, he remained very close to Trina and her father, preferring to walk between them if he could; but he seemed to be taking in everything with great interest.

Even stranger was what happened during the thunderstorms – Pats talked. His father had predicted that he would talk, but Trina was quick to notice that it was only during the storms that it happened. During the sunny spells he lapsed into his old silence. When he did talk, it wasn't at all like someone who had never talked before; everything he said was perfectly clear, although it didn't seem to connect with anything that was going on at the time. "I must hurry," he said on one occasion. On another, he said, "Well, it's not my fault either," in a distinctly sulky voice.

Trina realized that this happened only when the storm was directly above their heads; always just after the thunder and the lightning had come together. She whispered this discovery to her father, who muttered something about "electric shock treatment".

As evening came on, the storms stopped coming, and Pats returned to his familiar "absent" self, staring vacantly off into space, while one of his hands gently stroked the other.

They went back to the place where Trina's

father was living. Trina noticed then that there seemed to be largish groups of young men standing at many of the street corners. They had an air of restless expectancy. "What are they waiting for?" Trina asked, as they crossed the road to avoid one especially large group.

"I don't know," her father said. "I don't know what's going on. I don't think I like the look of it though."

The place Trina's father had rented had once been a carpenter's workshop ("just the right place to rebuild a boat," he remarked), and at the back of the main part of the shed there were three rooms: a toilet, and two other rooms which had been offices but which were now a bedroom and a kitchen. It was all very bare and unhomely, with the wallpaper coming off the walls in places and dirty dishes stacked in the tiny sink, but at the same time it was quite exciting. Trina and Pats had brought sleeping-bags, and her father had managed to get a couple of camp-beds from someone at the university. They were going to be eating a take-away supper out of tinfoil dishes; and no one would expect them to get washed before they went to bed.

All three of them would be sleeping in the one room, but Trina's father said he would be working late on the Burial Ship, so she and Pats would be able to get to sleep without his disturbing them. It was a pity, she felt, that the thunderstorms seemed to have passed; she had been hoping for the chance of a private conversation with Pats.

Her father's Ship stood in the shed, already looking quite like a proper boat, sitting in a row of great U-shaped cradles he had borrowed from somewhere down at the docks. All the timbers he had been able to find had now been brought back to the shed, all numbered and ready to go into their place. But of course where the dragon-prow should have butted on to the massive keel, there was an empty space.

Trina helped her father a little after supper, while Pats wandered about the shed poking at pieces of wood. But it had been a long day, with visits to a funfair, journeys through endless shops that Trina wanted to see, and a trek through the harbour area to see the big ships. She was soon nodding off, standing on her feet as she was. For a while after wriggling into their sleeping-bags it seemed they wouldn't sleep, because of the strangeness of the place. Pats lay on his back staring at a brown patch on the ceiling. "I suppose everything's a bit strange for you, Pats," Trina said; and fell asleep.

She jerked awake again. She peered at her watch and saw it was past midnight, though her father was not in bed yet. Pats was still lying on his back, with his eyes closed now.

Dimly, somewhere behind the endless rumbling of the city – how long it seemed now since that had been a familiar, nightly noise! – Trina realized there was some sort of distant commotion. It was hard to make out exactly what it was. There was a queer jerkiness about the sound, but little more than that. She slipped out of her sleeping-bag and crawled over the creaking camp-bed to the door of the little room.

Her father was not by the boat, but was standing at the big double door of the shed, which was slightly open. She padded across the cold concrete floor and stood behind him. "What's happening?" she asked.

"I don't know," he said. He fell silent, looking grim. "It's this rioting," he went on at last. "It spreads, you see, from one city to another. And there are people too, who just go about from city to city and start riots."

"Why? Who?"

He sighed. "Angry people, I suppose. Just angry. We move out to Newborough to get away from all that, and what happens? The very first night you come back here, it all starts again."

Trina wondered if he was saying it was her fault.

"It's a sign of the times, that's all," he said.

"What do they do, when they riot?"

He shrugged. "Break. Burn. Make a lot of

noise. Smash up shops and steal things out of them. Turn cars over and set light to them. If there's people they don't like the look of … well…" He fell silent.

She shuddered. She was sure she wouldn't be able to sleep now. Was this really going on here, now?

She had just crawled back into her sleeping-bag when she heard the rustle of Pats' head turning in the bed next to her.

"Who are you?" Pats said.

"Trina," said Trina, and waited.

Pats sighed deeply. "Are you Kittel's sister?" he said at last.

"Whose sister?" said Trina, as her heart began to thump, fast.

"Kittel's," Pats repeated.

How could Pats possibly know about Kitty? "I had a sister called Kitty," Trina said unsteadily.

"It's because of the barrier," Pats whispered. "Puckel said there was a barrier. Like the wall of mist. It's because you don't hear things properly when you're dreaming. There's a game Kittel told me about—"

"Chinese whispers," Trina said. Of course, she and Kitty used to play it with their friends, years ago, by candlelight…

There was a long pause. At last Pats said, "There's a bridge being built."

"What sort of bridge?" Trina asked.

"A bridge so she can get home. No – more than that. I think it's a bridge for us all to get over; for something ... from the Giants' Door ... to get over."

"Where is she?" Trina breathed.

"She's lost at the moment," Pats said. "But I'm sure she's all right."

"When will the bridge be made?" Trina asked.

"Not long now, I don't think," Pats replied.

"Where does it go from?"

"The Scroll Cupboard, I think."

"I know where that is," said Trina. "I've been there."

"Have you?" Trina heard Pats sitting up in the darkness. "Do you know the Secret Way?"

"I – I'm not sure," Trina faltered. "I went along the old railway line—"

"The old railway line!" Pats burst out. "Oh! So it really did come here, all the way... It's buried at our end."

"I don't know what you mean," said Trina. "I met Mother Egg – perhaps you know her too? And she showed me the Scroll Cupboard."

"Is she a person?" Pats enquired.

"Yes, of course."

"What's she like?"

Trina described her.

Pats let out a soft whistle. "That's Ms Minn," he said. "I just know it is. She used to be our teacher. She is a person – in a way. But she's the place too – the place of power. And I bet it's the same with King Puck! I bet that's Puckel – that's where he's hiding when I can't find him."

Trina was silent. She was too amazed to speak.

Her father burst into the room at that moment. "You two," he said tensely, "I want you to get up and get dressed. It's certainly a riot. There are buildings burning. And I think it's coming this way. We're getting out of here."

As Trina and Pats hurriedly dressed, Trina, who scarcely noticed the excitement of what was going on outside because of the excitement she felt within herself, turned suddenly to Pats and said, "Pats – that's not your real name, is it?"

"I'm called Sparrow," said Pats.

"Can you fly?" Trina said, and giggled, despite herself, because what she had asked seemed so silly.

But Pats replied gravely, "Only at night, I think. I'm actually dreaming just now."

14

ON THE
MOUNTAIN-TOP

Kittel and Bull were near the end of the long,
gradual climb over the rock-strewn ground on
the west side of the Valley of Murmuring
Water. They were in sight of the forests which
lay all around the skirts of the great, humped
mountain which formed one end of the Copperhill valley. Kittel was hoping to get into the
shelter of the forest before night came on, but
there were still several miles to go, and the day-
light was already failing.

"What's that funny light?" she said suddenly, pointing over to their left.

"Probably the sunset," Bull said. "I don't
see anything special."

"It's not," Kittel said presently. "It's coming
from those trees, down in that hollow."

Bull shrugged, and let his pony plod on.

"I'm going down to look," Kittel said.

"Wait for me. It may be a good place to spend the night."

Bull tutted, but drew in his reins and waited, watching as Kittel climbed off her pony and led it down the rough slope towards the hollow. He saw her standing at the edge and then leaving her pony as she plunged into some bushes. He stared, at a loss. He couldn't follow her there, either on foot or on his pony.

Kittel had found where the light was coming from. It was a hawthorn tree, in full blossom, quite ordinary – except that it was haloed in a rose-white glow. As she approached it, its young, bright-green leaves began to rustle, even though there was no breeze. She stopped. There was something uncanny about the little tree. She glanced back and saw, between the leaves at the edge of the hollow, Bull waiting where she had left him on his pony.

"He must come too," came Puckel's voice. "You are the only two who have known this thing."

Kittel turned, and saw the old man sitting at the foot of the tree with his hands resting on his stick, which was upright in front of him. He had not been there a moment ago, she was perfectly sure.

"He can't walk," Kittel said hoarsely.

"Course he can," Puckel snorted, "he's just being a booby." He hauled himself to his feet, using the stick as a prop. "Come on down!"

he roared up to Bull. "You can't stay there all night!"

Bull had very little option. The sound of Puckel's voice echoed against the mountains like thunder, and Bull's pony promptly reared up on its hind legs and threw him off. But before Kittel had even time to feel concerned, he had scrambled to his feet, cast a dirty glance at the wide-eyed pony, and come running down the slope towards them.

He burst through the bushes at the edge of the hollow. "It's better!" he exclaimed. "My ankle's mended! I..." Then he saw Puckel, turned white, and fell silent.

"Turn round, both of you," Puckel ordered. They obeyed, and the next moment they felt themselves gripped at the back of the neck, and were rocketing up into the air. Both shut their eyes and gritted their teeth and wished it would stop.

It did, quite soon. They landed on the top of a mountain. The freezing wind of evening, blowing off the heights, curled itself round them.

Kittel at once recognized the place, which Sparrow had described to her after his last visit there. Behind the low wall between two of the brightly-decorated buildings she saw the ruins of the aeroplane she herself had travelled in. She had never before been back here. She shivered.

"You, young Bull," Puckel said. "Do you know why I have brought you here?"

Bull shook his head.

"Well," Puckel went on, with a mysterious look on his wrinkled, unsmiling face, "there's a change to be made – a switch-over, you might call it."

Bull and Kittel watched as the old man turned and took a few steps, looking round at the dark triangle-entrances of the small buildings. He swung his stick and then, quite carelessly it seemed, sent it flying over and over to land inside one of them. He rubbed his face, as if tired. "Well," he said, "everything's ready. Now it's just a case of waiting for something to happen."

"What did you mean, only Bull and I have known something?" Kittel asked.

"Well," Puckel said, blowing out his cheeks in the rather sly way he sometimes had. "Bull's in a bit of a unique position really, isn't he? Him and the dragon, you know."

Bull stirred, and looked uneasy. He and Kittel both knew what the old man was meaning – that disastrous week, three years ago, when Bull had had some of the magic powers that later passed to Sparrow. It had resulted in the dragon taking Bull's shape for a short time.

"Puckel," said Kittel. "You know the dragon's going about in the shape of a cat, and we couldn't work out how—"

"Yes, yes," Puckel interrupted her. "I was coming to that. One thing at a time."

Kittel fell silent. The air was growing darker now. Too quickly, it seemed, just to be the oncoming of night.

"It is time things were explained to you a little," Puckel said. "Explained to you, and through you on to Sparrow. I think you've all deserved it. You have, on the whole, done your work pretty well, and I'm moderately pleased with you."

"*You're* hardly one to talk," came a voice. Bull and Kittel looked sharply round, to see an old, frail-looking woman sitting in the triangle of the doorway where Puckel had thrown his stick.

Bull turned pale for a second time. "Ms – Ms Minn…" he stammered.

The old schoolteacher did not stir. "No need to be afraid of me now, Bull," came the dry, cracked voice. "What's past is past. The things you did wrong you had to do – there was no one else to do them."

The last time Bull had seen Ms Minn was when he had had magic powers and had foolishly tried to shift into her shape.

Puckel, who had actually looked a little embarrassed when the old woman first spoke, had collected himself again. "We waited many years," he said, "many, many years for one to waken up and understand that he was living in the dream of the dragon – the dragon, Ureychyoburenitho, who lay beneath the mountain and dreamed of all that was going on in the world. So many stupid, dough-brained folk, living their foolish lives and never thinking to look up and stop and wonder. Eventually one did; and that was Bull – Bull who woke up to the power that is sometimes called magic."

And now the night had gathered around them, and Kittel and Bull could see nothing of Puckel. But only a moment after she had realized it was completely dark, Kittel became aware of a growing light on the eastern horizon.

"As to that power," Puckel went on, "it is something people don't see; it comes from they don't know where. Magic is like the wind blowing – you see the trees bending and the leaves and dust flying, but you do not see the wind itself. This wind comes from the centre of the earth, from the Door – the Giants' Door."

Suddenly Kittel, who had been watching the light grow at unbelievable speed in the eastern sky, interrupted. "Puckel!" she exclaimed. "There's that cat!"

Sitting in the doorway where Ms Minn had been a moment before, and looking demure as anything, was the black cat from the Hollywell. Only now there was something different about it...

"It's not the dragon any more," Kittel whispered, peering hard at the creature in what was now the light of a grey morning. "It's – it's…"

"Yes?" Puckel prompted. "What do you see?"

"Nothing," said Kittel in a puzzled voice. "I mean, I know that something's there, something's taken the cat's shape, but I can't see what. It's a complete blank."

"Good," said Puckel. "You are one of the few who have seen something of the hidden powers of the Door. Let me introduce you to Mother Egg. Despite appearances, Mother Egg is not a cat; the cat, in his way, is just an ordinary mog – he happens to be one of a small group of slightly eccentric creatures who let themselves be used by the rest of us, when there's a need." He glanced at Bull. "So," he said, nodding, "switch-over completed."

"So where's the dragon?" said Kittel.

"Ah, now that's a bit of a complication," Puckel replied. "I think we'll leave the dragon for the moment – though as I've no doubt you've guessed, the dragon is the other hidden power. Where Mother Egg is nothing, the dragon Ureychyoburenitho is – or should I say the Star Wheel is, for along with the dragon you have the Polymorphs, as you know—"

"This is unnecessarily complicated," the dry voice of Ms Minn broke in. "You're simply trying to avoid telling the tale of your own foolishness."

Looking over in her direction, Kittel and

Bull still saw only the black cat. But its little pink mouth was open when Ms Minn's voice spoke, and closed when it stopped. That could only mean that Ms Minn and the mysterious Mother Egg were one and the same, though Kittel couldn't understand why she wasn't able to see the old woman in the cat's shape.

Puckel gave a deep sigh, then pursed his lips, then made a dreadful grimace as if he were trying to come to a difficult decision. "All right," he said at length. "All right, I'll do it. I said I would."

For Kittel and Bull, who so far had heard only of Puckel's power and strength, a story of his foolishness was something quite new, and they listened agog. As the old man spoke, the sky darkened and paled, darkened and paled, as the light of a grey day was followed by the blackness of deep night, over and over again. Seven times the sky darkened and paled, though they didn't think to count it.

Far down in the Valley of Murmuring Water, Ormand and Lissie dug and waited, dug and waited; and Sparrow came and went, carefully removing the fragile, shimmering dragon bones from the tunnel beneath the valley floor. A vacant, faraway expression was on his face, as though his mind were somewhere else; and through the whole of that seven days, not a word did he speak to either of his friends.

And at the same time, but all in the one night, Trina and Pats shivered in the chill air of after-midnight and peered into the night of the city, where the sky was reddened with the burning of buildings. And all at once, Pats gave an exclamation. "The goats!" he said. "I have to find the goats!"

15

CHAOS

"Are they coming this way?" Trina asked.

"Hard to say," her father answered. "But I don't want to be caught on the hop if they do."

"What'll we do?"

"Stay put," her father said, "and keep all the lights off. Don't do anything to attract attention. It's public property they'll attack first, or anything that looks valuable. So if we're not a hi-fi shop or a police station or a pub, they'll probably pass us by. But if things look bad, the van's out at the back, and there's enough small, quiet streets for us to make a getaway. If it comes to that, I want you to keep hold of Pats' hand and stay close to me."

Trina nodded. The braying and skirling of sirens were coming from all directions now. And over the rising tumult from the city a wind seemed to be getting up, swirling dust and pieces of rubbish along the pavement.

"We'd better shut the door now," her father said, "and get to the other end of the shed."

"The goats!" Pats exclaimed suddenly. "I have to find the goats!"

Trina's father, who was just closing the door, stared at him. "Well, you do choose your moments—"

"He started speaking again just before you got us up," Trina said. "It's not really Pats at all, you know."

Her father ushered them down to the other end of the shed. Trina was about to explain what she had meant, when they heard the vibration of a heavy engine outside the door they had just closed, and saw lights through the small, grimy windows.

"Stay where you are," Trina's father said, and went back to the door to look. After a minute or two, they saw him hurriedly opening the door and speaking urgently with someone outside. A minute later, five or six strangers pushed through into the shed, including a man with a peaked cap carrying a small grey box under his arm.

It turned out to be the driver of the last bus of the night with a handful of scared-looking passengers. The road ahead was blocked, the driver said, and he had backed the bus into the entrance of the shed meaning to turn it round, but in his hurry he had got it stuck against the low wall just outside. Trina's father had signalled to him to come in and bring his passengers.

It seemed like a crowd to Trina. There was a woman of about her mother's age, with two small, bleary-looking children clutching her coat; a young man and two older men, all drunk; and an old woman who appeared to be very dirty and was clutching a snarling Pekinese under her arm. The driver was the only one among them who looked as though he would be any use in an emergency.

Trina's father was trying to assure the bemused visitors – who were gazing stupidly at the half-built ship – that they would be safe, when a roar came from outside. They started in alarm as something heavy struck the door of the shed, and a commotion of bangings, thumpings and yellings began. The two little children started whimpering.

"We have to go now," Pats said, with urgency in his voice. But no one moved.

"They're going for the bus," said the bus-driver at length.

He had hardly spoken when there was a roar that rattled the doors and windows, and a burst of orange light outside. Black smoke began to pour under the shed door.

"Just in time, mate – thanks," the bus-driver said.

Trina's father was not listening. With an

exclamation he had started towards the double doors again. Trina quickly realized what was on his mind. The burning bus was against them, and piled next to them on the inside were the remaining timbers of the Ship. Trina sprang after her father, who was now frantically hauling at the tinder-dry planks and post. Already, yellow flames were licking greedily at the bottom edge of the doors.

The people from the bus, meanwhile, forgotten by Trina and her father, were shifting uneasily. "This way, please," Pats said suddenly, and walked through the midst of them, through the little kitchen and to the back door of the shed. There was a moment of confused shuffling, and then the people, led by the old woman with the Pekinese, followed him one by one. Pats opened the door at the back of the van.

It was soon obvious to Trina that it was no use. She could feel the heat of the fire through the doors. Her father's face was pouring with sweat in the red light. In a moment the doors were going to go up. Still he was heaving and hauling. One of the more badly-rotted planks cracked, and her father cursed, scrabbling at the long timber to try and hold it together.

"Where's Pats gone?" said Trina suddenly.

"What?" her father looked up, a savage expression on his face. "Where is he?"

"I don't know!" Trina wailed. "The people have gone as well!"

Woomph! The doors took fire, and flames enveloped them on the inside.

"Oh damn, damn, damn!" her father roared. "All that work! All that precious history!" Then after a moment's agonized hesitation he grabbed Trina's arm and rushed her through the shed to the open back door.

He was a little taken aback to see Pats and all the people from the bus piled into the back of the van. "A lot they could care," he muttered as he climbed into the driver's seat.

Trina wondered who had got them all organized. Not Pats, surely? She could see at a glance that he had once again become his old "absent" self. He sat gazing fixedly at a point in the middle of the old woman's chest, while her dog seemed to be trying to stretch out its squashed-up nose towards him. Not much chance of it smelling anything but its mistress, Trina thought to herself, as she wound down the window.

Her father was right about the streets at the back of the shed. In fact it seemed that, whoever the rioters were who had come up their road, they were not really at the centre of the trouble. Along at the ends of the streets they crossed there seemed to be crowds of people running, throwing things, milling together, dark figures against the lurid orange glow of burning.

They were heading towards the city centre,

not out towards Newborough. It seemed that all the people from the bus lived on the other side of the city and were anxious to get back to their homes. Only the ragged old woman seemed to be unconcerned, and made growling noises into the Pekinese's ear.

But as they came nearer to the city centre, things began to get worse and worse.

"No use," Trina's father said, driving the van into a street off a large concourse, and then quickly reversing out again as a line of policemen appeared at the far end, facing away from them but retreating towards them.

"Go down that way," the bus-driver said, pointing to another street. All the streetlights were out here – Trina saw jagged edges of broken glass on one of them – but there were no fires and no people. The van's headlights swung into the sullen darkness. It was not until they had rounded a bend towards the far end that they found their way blocked by two cars lying upside down. By the time they had turned in the narrow street and driven back to the top end, the policemen and a crowd of stone-throwers were swarming in all directions over the concourse. Trina's father backed down the full length of the street again, grazing lamp-posts and parked cars in his haste.

"It's no use," he repeated, as they came to a stop before the two wrecked cars. "We'll have to get out of here and get indoors."

They decided they should all make a run for the bus-driver's sister's house, which was not far away. Unwillingly, everyone piled out into the dark street. One of the drunk men immediately set off in the direction of the trouble, and would pay no heed to the driver's warnings. The two little girls' whimpering had become a constant, low-pitched gibber. They, and all the others, obediently followed the bus-driver, but just as Trina turned to grab Pats' hand, she saw the old woman come up behind him and give him an almighty kick up the rear. What Pats would normally have done Trina didn't know, but what happened just now was that he sailed into the air and seemed to hover there for a second, before falling lightly down on his feet again in front of her. Pats grinned, and Trina knew that the boy, Sparrow – whatever he was – was back. "You must find your own way," he said quietly to her. "I have to find the goats."

"What?" said Trina. "What?" But Pats turned away from her and went to stand beside her father. She glanced round. No one else seemed to have noticed the old woman's extraordinary behaviour, or the fact that Pats had actually flown up into the air. They were filing between the two upended cars while her father counted them through. "Keep right behind me," he said to her as she came up. Cautiously, they set off after the bus-driver between the high, dark buildings.

Almost immediately, Trina heard the wail of "Leechee, where have you gone?" She turned, somehow knowing it was the voice of the dirty old woman. It was coming from behind the cars, although Trina had seen her going through the gap with the others. What was she up to? She was just the kind of old wretch who would be nothing but trouble. She seemed to be down on her hands and knees behind the car.

Of course, she *would* have to go and lose her dog! Trina hesitated, looking after her father striding behind the bedraggled group from the bus, then ran back to the old woman. "Where did he go?" she said.

"I don't know, dash him," the crone bellowed in her ear. "He gave me the slip, the little garbage-can, the little flea-bag, he's always giving me the slip, and now look what he's gone and done!"

"You'll have to come," Trina said urgently. "He – he'll probably follow, he can't be far. Anyway, I'm sure he can look after himself better than we can, and we've got to get on." She was feeling she ought to get hold of her and drag her with her, but she didn't like the thought of touching the old creature.

"Oh, you don't understand – you don't understand!" the woman began to howl. "I can't leave him, he's everything to me, he's my only friend, he's – oh, there! Look, there he is!

Quick, run and get him, dearie – oh, be quick, please!"

What was Trina to do? The others were already out of sight... But the street was so dark it was hard to make anything out except by the faint glow of the distant concourse; if they lost sight of the dog there was little chance of finding it again...

Trina made a dash for it. After all, it couldn't get far on those stumpy little legs, hidden under such a thick mat of hair...

16

A BOOT UP THE REAR

Sparrow blinked. How long had he been sitting here, looking at Ms Minn? There she sat, watching him fixedly, with a cold, distant look in her eyes. He frowned, shook himself, glanced around.

They were in the Scroll Cupboard; but there was something different about the light. It was no longer dim and silver-grey, but bright, with a special brightness like the sky before sunrise. He soon saw the reason – a part of the wall and a part of the low-arching roof had disappeared, and he could see a blue-green sky streaked with long, pale-yellow clouds.

And then he saw the bridge. In one clean, incredible arch it curved from the floor of the Scroll Cupboard into the sky – up, over and down, down out of sight. He scrambled to his feet and went over to the opening in the wall.

And then he gasped.

There was a whole world down there – a world of woods, fields, hills, rivers, towns. It wasn't spread out flat below him, but seemed to be tipped at an angle towards him – or else it was flat and he and the Scroll Cupboard were at an angle. It was all very still and quiet, shadowy-green. The great bridge of dragon bones arched like a rainbow from where he stood down to where a great pyramid-shaped mountain rose in the very centre of the wide land he saw. At the top of its curve the bridge must have caught the sunlight, for there it sparkled like a dazzling jewel.

"Did I do all that?" said Sparrow wonderingly. "While I was there, in the other place? How long have I been asleep?" For that was how it felt to him, even though the memory of the shed with the ancient boat, and the burning, and the frightened people in the van, was clearer than any dream could be.

"Don't be a fool," came the dry voice of Ms Minn behind him. "This is no time to congratulate yourself. Look at your feet."

But Sparrow, surprised, looked round. It was Ms Minn who was sitting there, sure enough, but the voice had been unmistakably the voice he had last heard coming from the scorpion – the voice of Puckel's stick. "Look at your feet," Ms Minn said again, with an edge of threat in her tone; and Sparrow did as he was told.

The first two dragon bones lay lightly on the sand and stones of the floor, just in front of his boots. But the next bone was not attached to them. There was a gap before the main part of the bridge started. Not a big gap; a gap of about one dragon bone's length.

"The bridge is not complete," Ms Minn remarked, "because of your tomfoolery."

"The third bone," said Sparrow in a low voice. "You mean there were just enough bones – not a single one more?"

"There was no room for error," Ms Minn confirmed. "Now only one creature can complete the bridge, and that is the one creature that must not be allowed to cross it."

"The dragon," said Sparrow dully. "But I still don't understand—"

"Nobody asked you to understand," Ms Minn said. "Only to do." There was a short silence before she went on again. "What you see below you is not the world as it is, but the world as it might have been if the dragon had not spoiled it. A green world, a world at peace with itself. A dream of the world, a possibility. If the dragon crosses the bridge again, it will be to complete the destruction it began."

"What can I do?" said Sparrow. "I'll do anything to put it right."

"You will not pay the price for your mistake," said Ms Minn.

"But I want to," said Sparrow. "I really do—"

"Silence," Ms Minn said sharply. "That's not for you to choose. Look at me, boy – look at me closely."

Sparrow, who had been gazing out of the opening in the wall, turned to look at Ms Minn again. It seemed that his old teacher was just as he remembered her; but as he looked now, he saw that there was something different. At first he thought she was fading – as he had seen her do once before – but she was still perfectly visible. Yet as he looked it seemed to him more and more as if she had turned to glass; not completely clear glass, but glass that was just clear enough to look through, if you put your mind to it. And Sparrow saw what seemed to be a pool of water, with ripples in circles out from its centre – except that the ripples were the coils of a red-and-brown snake; and the coils of the snake were the hard, brittle twists of the wood of Puckel's stick. And there was the scorpion too, deep in the centre of the pool, with its evil sting poised above its back; and in the midst of the scorpion was a tiny egg; and inside the egg a darkness that Sparrow presently realized was the night-sky full of its countless stars.

"Yes," Ms Minn said. "You have seen correctly. That old gas-bag that you called Ms Minn is no more – and no less – than the outer shell of Mother Egg. And I have no choice either. You must do what it's your job to do, and others must suffer to put right your mistakes."

Sparrow bowed his head. It seemed such a small mistake – made for what seemed good reasons at the time – yet it seemed it could have such enormous consequences.

"In this last week you have been able to come and go as you please," said Mother Egg. "Now, for the bridge to be completed in the right way, you must cross it from where you do not belong to where you do belong. There is only one way for you to come back to the mountains of the Giants' Door – across the completed bridge. If the bridge is completed in the wrong way – through being crossed from this side – you will not be able to return. You will wither away inside the shell of the boy you are down in that place. So you are a hostage of our success. So is the girl. She will remain here until you have completed the bridge. Tell her she must find her own way. And tell the man who makes a boat out of the splinters of my spinning-wheel that there is one piece missing which must be found. You have the Secret Way with you, and the Masters of the Dragon's Dreaming are stirring up nightmare in the dark pit they call a city. And that is all as it should be. Now go."

"I don't know if I can find the way back,"

said Sparrow humbly.

"You must follow the goats," said Mother Egg. "Turn round again. I shall send you."

Sparrow had barely turned back to the opening in the wall when he felt the force of Ms Minn's leather boot lifting him off his feet and high, high, impossibly high into the air.

17

THE NIGHTMARE
STATUE

"Back up to the concourse," Trina's father yelled. "It's the only way she can have gone."

Sparrow ran with him, up the dark street, between the toppled cars.

"Here, into the van," Trina's father gasped. "We'll take it as long as we can get through."

The concourse was complete pandemonium. There were people everywhere, yelling, running, rolling about fighting, throwing things, waving things, breaking things. There were no buildings burning here, but somewhere behind they could see a great spout of spark-lit smoke rising and billowing wildly in the hot wind. Could Trina possibly be here? Surely not.

Her father climbed onto the roof of the van and gazed about feverishly. At that moment Sparrow saw the statue of the Sphinx – a great stone lion-shape, paws outstretched and head erect, the stone mane cropped in the shape of a bell, and the human face with faraway eyes and faintly-smiling mouth.

But it was not a statue. It was a Polymorph. That is to say, it was a Polymorph hiding in the statue. Sparrow had long ago received a wound in his left eye, which was how he could see the things of the Secret Way if he wanted to. This Polymorph was hiding in the stone Sphinx, but it couldn't hide from his seeing eye. The stone shape was like a shadow enclosing the humped, vulture-like form of the creature; its small dark eyes gloated from behind the unseeing stone ones.

The Polymorphs had not been allowed out of the Secret Way and the Star Wheel for well over a year now. There was something crazy about seeing one of them here in the city – and yet ... perhaps it wasn't crazy at all. What were those words of Mother Egg's – about the Secret Way and the Masters of the Dreaming being with him? Was it possible he could have brought the creatures with him – that somehow the Secret Way had opened out into this strange place, and they could create madness here, stir up nightmare, just as they had done once before, in the mountains?

Trina's father was looking away. Sparrow skipped into the air and rose effortlessly up to stand on the ledge beside the Sphinx's mane.

The stone eye seemed to roll round at him. "You're the Polymorph Eni," Sparrow said coldly. "You're doing all this to the people – you're the cause of it all."

The Polymorph seemed quite untroubled. "You want my head?" it said in its dull, sneering voice. "Take it. See what happens."

Sparrow hesitated. He knew that the huge stone head of the sphinx was only the dreaming, and the real thing was the Polymorph's tall, domed head, which he could easily remove. He had done so, once before. That would certainly put the Polymorph out of action, though he didn't know if he would be able to return the head to the Star Wheel. Possibly he could seek out all the Polymorphs here, and take their heads, and everything would immediately calm down in this city. But Mother Egg had said that what they were doing here was "all as it should be".

Sparrow decided he couldn't dare to interfere or again do something he had not been told to do. Whatever trouble the Polymorphs were causing here, it was all part of what was happening – it might even be a part of the finishing of the bridge.

"No," he said. "No, I don't want your head. But I want goats. I'm looking for goats. Where are they?"

"All sheep here," said the smiling Sphinxmouth. "No goats, just sheep. Look."

Sparrow looked down at the seething crowd. They were a bit like sheep – sheep scrambling madly to get through a gate, sheep caught in a hopeless tangle of brambles, struggling endlessly, uselessly, stupidly…

"Pats! What in heaven's name are you doing up there?" came the voice of Trina's father. "Will you come down! At once!"

Sparrow turned, and jumped from the ledge to the ground below. "Sorry," he said.

"Things are bad enough as they are without you getting yourself into trouble," his companion scolded. "Now keep by me."

Sparrow did as he was told, though he was aware that the Polymorph Eni was jeering at him from the statue. He ignored it. He decided that if Trina's father was searching for Trina, and he himself was searching for goats, and neither of them had any idea how to find what they were searching for, they might as well search together.

They searched. Through the roaring streets, through the hot wind with its cargo of dust and ash and sparks and fearful smells of burning, through the orange glare and the dark eerie shadows, through the screams and the sudden silences, through the surging crowds and the empty streets. Sometimes they went in the van, sometimes on foot. The van was never touched, even though they left it unlocked when they got out to hunt among the streets they couldn't drive into. And they came to no harm, either from the rioters or from the scores and hundreds of police who were now appearing from every side. The recklessness of despair seemed to protect Trina's father. It was obvious from the start that they had little chance of finding Trina; but finding Trina was the thing he had set out to do, and he didn't seem to care about anything else. He took risks, and no harm came to them. On one occasion something hard hit him on the side of the head. He scarcely noticed. He brushed the blood away with his hand and strode on, while Sparrow trotted beside him.

When Sparrow had been in the city earlier in the day, and glimpsed through Pats' eyes the ordinary traffic and crowds, he had been fascinated, but terrified, by all its strangeness. Now, in some strange way, with the Polymorphs here with him in the city, he felt comforted. He didn't like them or trust them, but he was used to their madness – it belonged to his world; it was a link with the Mountains, and Mother Egg, and Puckel.

18

THE OLD RIDDLE

Puckel took a deep breath. "Very well," he said, "I shall tell the tale of my foolishness." He gazed out over Kittel's and Bull's heads to the darkening and brightening sky.

"Long, long ago," he began, "years and years and more time than even I care to think of, I was a young lad, curious and not very wise. And one day when my master, Obyr, was away, I was wandering about in my loafish way, peering and poking into things that didn't concern me and generally trying to find out more than a young fellow should.

"And so I came to Mother Egg, and stood on the edge of the great abyss that has no bottom, and wondered if it could be crossed, and what would lie on the far side if it were crossed.

"And as I stood and wondered, up came the

dragon, Ureychyoburenitho, slithering and steaming. 'Would you like to build a bridge across, little Puka?' he asked. 'How can I do that?' I said. 'Easy,' said Ureychyoburenitho. 'You must let me ask you a question which you cannot answer.' 'That should be easy enough,' I agreed. 'What's the question?' 'The question is this,' said Ureychyoburenitho: 'Are the things of the world there because I dream them, or do I dream them because they are there?' 'I don't know,' said I, without thinking. 'Not good enough,' said he. 'You must try to find the answer.' For three days and nights I sat and tried to think of the answer, and I knew I shouldn't, because Obyr had told me I should engage in no conversations with the dragon. But as the three days passed, I became more and more curious to know what the answer was to his riddle, and I forgot about the bridge over the abyss.

"But at the end of the three days Ureychyoburenitho came back and asked me: 'Have you found the answer?' 'No,' I said. 'What is the answer?' 'I never said I would tell you it,' said he, 'but thanks for the bridge.' And with that he arched over the abyss like a rainbow. And as his nose touched the far side, I had a vision of a world that was spoiled with ash and smoke, where the plants withered and the animals died and the people went mad. And I knew that Ureychyoburenitho had cheated me and broken the balance of the Giants' Door.

"When Obyr returned, he was very angry. But when he had finished being angry he was distressed, and for three days he sat and wept. And when he had finished weeping he sat for three days more and thought. And when he had finished thinking he put out all of his power, and made certain changes to the Giants' Door that would one day lead to the recapturing of Ureychyoburenitho. But at the same time he said that the bridge Ureychyoburenitho had made could never be unmade, and that the power of the Door would always pass across a bridge of dragon bones.

"So Obyr exhausted all his strength, and he left us, and I took his place in King Puck at the head of the Door, and my sister was in the place of Mother Egg. And from seven scales which Ureychyoburenitho had left behind in the Star Wheel there came the Masters of the Dragon's Dreaming – the Polymorphs. And when I had grown older and a little wiser, I saw that we still had time to act, because the power of the loosened dragon was growing only slowly. So then we – I, my sister and the Masters of the Dreaming – shaped the mountain-country as a shell in which to hide the Giants' Door, and in the course of time brought people from the world to live among the mountains, to live simply and without change, free of the madness of the dragon. Though many thoughts of the dragon slipped over the bridge, none of them had any power—"

Bull was unable to contain himself. "That's not what Ms Minn told us!" he burst in. "She said there was a railway line, and the mountains were just an ordinary part of the world, and—"

"Well?" Puckel said, turning towards the black cat, with one bushy eyebrow raised. Kittel thought he looked rather delighted, and at the same time she was sure that the expression on the cat's face was, in its turn, rather embarrassed – if a cat ever can look embarrassed. At any rate, it suddenly started vigorously washing its face with its paw. "It was as true as it needed to be," Ms Minn's voice said at length, sounding slightly sulky.

"Huh," Puckel snorted, turning from the cat back to Bull and Kittel. "The railway line was no railway line at all – it was the bridge of dragon bones."

"What?" Bull burst in again. "It can't be! I know that railway line! I – we've walked on it! They've taken bits of it and melted it down and made things. My gran says our kitchen stove was made from the railway line—"

"That's right," Kittel interrupted him. "It's all like the dragon and the dragon bones – it doesn't make sense. One moment you say the dragon needs a bridge to cross over, and the next you say the dragon *is* the bridge; and

Ormand and Lissie dug up the dragon bones, and yet the dragon was still running about in the shape of that cat – I don't get it."

Puckel raised his hand, and Kittel fell silent. "You can't think of the dragon like an ordinary animal," he said. "Not like a fat old cow or an elephant, or anything like that. You can't exactly say, 'Here is a dragon', or, 'There goes a dragon', or, 'I've got a dragon in my garage'. You can't say, 'The dragon is dead', or, 'The dragon is alive and kicking and getting up to all sorts of mischief'. You can't say that kind of thing. The dragon is here, and there, and everywhere. His bones lie in the earth at the same time as he's flying through the air. He's a thousand little dragons and at the same time one whopping big dragon. You can't hold him down. And now everything that he has touched, every little drop of air that he has breathed, every little thought he has had, can turn into a dragon. Even your kitchen stove will spout flames when the wind tickles it the wrong way! But the world down there, beyond the mountains, where he breathed and sent all the people mad – it's full of dragons now, little ones and big ones, and they are all the one dragon.

"One thing holds the dragon back; one thing can check him, and that is Mother Egg. Little abysses for little dragons, big ones for big dragons. That was how it was all those years ago, when the trap we set for the dragon was Mother Egg herself in the form of a great lake – the same that you now call the Dead Lake. At the end of the dragon's freedom in the world, he devoured his own tail; in the frenzy of the madness he had stirred up he plunged into the abyss. After that, he could be trapped on the bridge of his own bones, which I then hid under the mountains."

Kittel and Bull still felt confused. Puckel's story was quite different from the story they knew – and yet, in some odd way, they could see it was the same story. "I suppose the dragon's just a confusing thing," Kittel said.

"You get used to him," Puckel said. "We've had longer than you to do that. If you can see he's confusing then you're off to a better start than I was. You'll do well. Even stupidity has its value. We've waited many years, trusting the day would come when out of these simple, stupid mountain-people one should appear who could put right what I had done wrong, rebuild the dragon bridge in a different form, and undo the madness and destruction which the dragon had brought."

"Sparrow," said Bull, a little bitterly. Puckel nodded.

"I never realized he was so special," Kittel murmured.

"He's not," said Puckel sharply. "And don't you go trying to let him think he is. Without

Bull, for example, where would he be? Still digging for pretty stones to give his mother, probably. Where would he be without his mother – or without you? Sparrow's only the seed; and you need a whole plant before you can have a seed.

"And now," he said, suddenly becoming brisk and businesslike, "it is time we had some action." He flung his tattered green coat on the ground. What was underneath was not much better, as clothes go. It was a brown tunic that showed his great, bare arms, brown and knotted with muscle, like oak branches. He swung round towards the doorway where the black cat still sat regarding him unblinkingly. "What you are about to see," he went on, "is the arrival here of the first little dragon from down yonder. It has come all the way just to disappear inside Mother Egg. Things are nearing completion."

Peering at the cat in the grey morning light, Kittel saw that in the nothingness inside it – the nothingness that was taking the cat's form – a tiny speck had appeared. The speck grew, and became a distant figure. Kittel narrowed her eyes. Bigger and more distinct the figure grew, until it seemed to be filling the whole shape of the cat. And then the outlines of the cat seemed to blur and fall apart – until at last, where the cat had been, head lowered to creep out of the small triangular doorway, there came a girl.

19

FOUNDATIONS

Little by little, the crowds seemed to be thinning. Buildings were still burning here and there, sirens were still wailing, but there was a definite feeling that the excitement was beginning to die down.

Now for the message, Sparrow thought – perhaps he'll pay attention now. They were in the van again, driving through almost deserted streets, swerving now and again to avoid piles of masonry or shattered glass or car wheels lying in their way. "There was a bit missing, from the boat," he said.

"The prow," Trina's father said shortly. "Probably shaped like a dragon's head."

"Ah," said Sparrow. Then: "You have to find it, you know."

Trina's father grunted. "Not much point now," he said. "Everything burned."

"You have to find it tonight," Sparrow said, very firmly.

Trina's father glanced briefly, strangely, across at Pats. "That's where it should be," he said, indicating a huge, dark area just beyond the pavement they were driving alongside.

There were the remains of a fence on the inside edge of the pavement, but the boards which had lined it were ripped away. In the half-darkness of the building site beyond, they could make out the criss-crossing lines of concrete foundations. At one end was a large mound of rubble and clay. "Somewhere in that pile of rubbish," Trina's father said.

Sparrow leaned across and put his hand on the steering wheel of the van. He had some vague idea he could slow the thing down if he touched the wheel. "You won't find Trina this way," he said. "You've got to find the missing part of the boat."

"Pats, get your hand off—" Trina's father was just beginning, when the van coughed, stuttered, and then jolted them forward in their seats. At the same moment, the headlights went off. They coasted forwards for a little, and came to a stop.

"Petrol? Electrics?" Trina's father muttered, running his hands through his already wild-looking hair.

Sparrow clambered out of the passenger door. "Come on," he said, and hopped across the pavement and over the edge of the drop down to the floor of the building site.

"Wait! Pats! Don't you dare go off! Come back here at once!" Trina's father spluttered. When he saw Pats taking no notice, he followed.

Sparrow waited for him at the last of the low foundation walls, near the mountain of rubble and clay. Trina's father seemed to have got over his angry outburst. He came and sat down on the wall near Sparrow. For a while he sat with his hands flopped between his knees, staring bleakly over the desolate site. Then he put his head down and hid his face in his hands. After a while he started shaking, as if with sobs.

"The very first time," he groaned. "The very first time she's left with me – and I go and lose her. I can't do anything right – I just can't do anything right. My whole life – I mess everything up. I lose Beth – now I've lost Kitty. What's wrong with me?

"Even the Ship," he went on. "What's become of it? A pile of ashes, that's what. Nothing left. That's what my life is – a pile of ashes."

Sparrow lifted his head and sniffed. There was a faintly familiar smell blowing towards him on the now lessening wind. He flared his nostrils, trying to get more of it, to make it out… A sweet, faintly sickly smell that made you wrinkle your nose and want to blow it out again…

That's what it was – billy-goat!

And round a corner of the street, into the light of the two street-lamps at the further end of the building site, the goats came trotting in a line.

There were nothing like as many as there had been on the mountain – twenty or thirty, maybe – but they looked outlandish enough in this strange, square, city-world. They were just as he had seen them before, heads down, jostling, clashing horns together, intent. They crossed the street, tripped onto the pavement, and without a pause jumped down onto the building site, where they came towards Sparrow and Trina's father, jumping over the low foundation walls in ones and twos, an undulating column. They looked dull orange in the weary light.

Trina's father let his hands fall and raised his head. But he wasn't looking towards the goats. He was staring off in the other direction, into the featureless city sky.

Just before they reached them, the goats stopped. Then the leader raised its head, shook its horns, looked directly at Sparrow, and bleated. Trina's father appeared not to notice. Suddenly the goat vanished.

Sparrow didn't feel at all surprised. He had seen something like this before, long ago. Far more important was the thought that came into his head at that moment. "What was your life, anyway?" he asked Trina's father. "What did you do? Were you a weaver?" (He was a little confused in his mind by what Mother Egg had said about the man making a boat out of her spinning-wheel.)

Trina's father frowned at him. "A weaver?" he said. "How do you work that out? I was an archaeologist. I don't think I'm anything now. I dug things up – old things – and examined them and tried to find out about the past – how people used to live, what they did…"

"Why?" said Sparrow.

"Why? Because the past's important, that's why. Because it tells us where we've come from. And perhaps that tells us a bit about where we're going to." He grunted. "Not that it makes much difference. I could have told you years ago where we're all going to. That's why I became an archaeologist. No one listens to you."

"Where are we all going?" asked Sparrow.

"Here," Trina's father said. "To places like this, in cities like this. Tonight. To destruction. To burning, looting…"

The two goats now at the front of the column raised their heads and bleated, then they too disappeared. Sparrow suddenly had another thought. He had been thinking of this strange man up to now as Trina's father – now he realized he was Kittel's father too. That seemed very queer. Then the thought struck him that apart from Kittel, this was the first person from this other world whom he'd had very much to do with. Ms Minn had told him ages ago that they were all mad in Kittel's place. He had never thought that Kittel was mad, but he was beginning to be fairly sure her father was.

Two more goats bleated, disappeared.

"I don't know who you are," Kittel's father said, looking straight at Sparrow. "I don't know what kind of world you've been living in all these years. 'In a world of his own' – that's what we said about you. Do you know what kind of world this is – the real world, I mean? It's a world where people put bombs on planes and kill everyone on board just so that other people in the world take some notice of them. They don't know the people they've killed. Never see them. They're just numbers. They're not people, to them. In the old days, the days of the Vikings, they were bad then too of course; but at least they killed people with their own hands – they looked into their eyes – they knew who they were killing…"

The wind was rising again. Bits of paper were buffeting across the low walls towards them. Shaggy goat-hair was stirring. Sparrow was not sure what was happening with the goats. They seemed to be bleating all the time now, raising their heads and disappearing, but there was always another in the place of the one which had just gone.

Suddenly Kittel's father gave a great howl, as if in rage or pain. He leaped to his feet and seized his hair in his hands, tugging at it violently. "It's gone far enough!" he yelled. "This is the end! It can't go on! Why can no one see it can't go on? They're all crazy – the whole world's gone mad! The whole world spoiled with ash and smoke – withering, dying! Freedom – they talk about freedom; what's freedom all about? They've let loose a dragon in the world – that's what their freedom's all about – a dragon that will destroy us all, destroy everything, until in the last frenzy of our madness it turns and devours its own tail!"

There was foam round his mouth, but as quickly as he had started raving he grew calm again. "And then," he said, in a quiet, but shaking voice, "then, if there's anything left, we'll have peace. At the end of everything."

There was one goat left. All the rest had disappeared.

Ideas, thoughts, a few good songs, a few good stories – no goats. That was what Puckel had said, and now Sparrow understood. Once, long before, when he had first been learning the Secret Way of the Mountains, Sparrow had sent a messenger to Bull without even knowing he was doing it. It had taken the form of a small Puckel-man. Even longer ago, he had seen Puckel himself turn into a whole menagerie of animals, and one of them – a goat – had given him a sort of message without words. It occurred to Sparrow that Puckel must be doing something like this the whole time. This strange, raving man in front of him was saying something important – something which came from thoughts which Puckel had sent to him. Somewhere out in the darkness of this city – or perhaps in the deeper darkness around the city – all those other goats would be going, taking thoughts, new songs, new stories, to people who were waiting to hear them. If this was what Puckel could do before the bridge had even been made, what could be done if they managed to complete it...?

The last goat was standing waggling its head in a foolish fashion, but it didn't bleat, and it didn't disappear.

"That's my goat," said Sparrow.

The goat disappeared.

Sparrow was watching Trina's father steadily. His hair was pulled all over the place by what his hands had been doing as he ranted and raved. But it wasn't just that; his hair was actually rising up from his scalp. And his eyes were staring upwards. He looked as though he had seen a ghost.

Sparrow suddenly realized he had risen off the ground and was floating in the air above the man. He wondered how that had happened. He grinned, and came lightly down to the ground again. "Sorry," he said. "I didn't mean to startle you."

Trina's father collapsed onto his knees. "Who are you?" he whispered.

"I'm called Sparrow," Sparrow answered. "I – I don't come from here. I come from somewhere else. I'm stuck here till I can get the bridge finished. If I don't, the dragon will come back. He's trying to. That may be why the Polymorphs are here, I don't know. They make people go mad – not just dangerous; they do silly things as well. You probably don't know what I mean."

"Oh, don't I?" Trina's father answered huskily. "No, I know exactly what you mean. But I think I'm going mad. I thought I saw you flying just now."

"I was," said Sparrow. "I can. All the time in my own place – I don't know if I can fly all the time here, though."

"And you need to find the dragon-prow to get back to your own place? Is that what you're saying?"

"I don't know if that is it exactly," Sparrow said. "It's just what Mother Egg said you had to do. I think it'll help, but I think there's something else that needs to be done at the other end, too."

Trina's father scrambled to his feet and dusted his knees with his hands. He shook his head. "It's impossible," he said. "It's lost. Gone. No idea where it could be. I've looked – believe me, I've looked."

"You've got to look again," Sparrow said.

"I've got to find Trina," her father said despairingly.

"She's all right," Sparrow said. "I've sent her off. She'll find her own way."

"Where?" breathed Trina's father.

"To my place. You'll see her again, but only if the bridge is finished."

"Are you threatening me?"

"No!" Sparrow chuckled. "No, I can't help it. She wanted to go – to find her sister."

"She doesn't have a sister."

"Doesn't she? Well, I know her sister. I met Trina once before, too – it was all a bit mixed up though. Anyway, we've got to get on. Are you coming?"

"I don't know if I'm coming or going," Trina's father muttered. "I'll show you the only place the prow might be."

They picked their way over to the mound of stones and clay. Dark, high, hopelessly huge, it loomed above them. "There," Trina's father said, flapping his hand towards it. "That's where it'll be. Can you burrow as well as fly?"

"It doesn't look much use," Sparrow agreed despondently. Then he took a jump towards the mound, flew up into the air and landed on top of it. The glow of a distant streetlight caught the side of his face as he gazed down over the shadowy building site.

"Incredible," Trina's father murmured.

"Absolutely incredible. Perhaps Trina wasn't imagining things after all. If boys can fly, there can be mountains that... Perhaps there is a change. Perhaps the world can change. Perhaps..." He tailed off. Then he said, in the same murmuring voice, "You're standing on its head. I'm not dreaming. You're standing on its head!" His voice rose.

"What?" the boy called down to him.

"Your foot! Look at your foot!" the man cried, starting to scramble up the slippery clay.

Sparrow looked down at his feet and saw something round. Bending down and peering, he found that it was a carved eye staring up at him from a strange-shaped, carved face. He saw a snarling mouth of spiky wooden teeth. He was standing on the neck. He stepped off and noticed the ground moving. The whole length of the lost prow lay there on the surface, buried under no more than a skim of clay.

Trina's father was scrabbling on the steep slope, and at last managed to crawl his way to the top just as Sparrow was clearing the mud from the head. "What a beauty," he murmured. "What a beauty."

The prow of the Burial Ship looked very dragon-like. It was not particularly the same shape as the head of the dragon which Sparrow had had dealings with, but there was something about its fearsome, intent expression that was just like the living dragon – it was a creature with a clear sense of direction.

Trina's father rocked the prow up and down a little with his foot. It seemed quite loose in the sticky soil and stones. "It's a miracle," he muttered. "I looked everywhere for it. And the digger must have dragged it to the top here when they were piling everything up. Can you give me a hand with it? I must get it to the van." He took hold of the neck and wiggled the prow slightly towards the edge of the mound.

Sparrow went to the other end and heaved, but he couldn't lift it. He could only rock it while Trina's father wiggled.

With a low groan of timber on stony earth, a yelp from Trina's father, and a skittering and clattering of slipping rubble, the prow slipped over the edge of the mound. Sparrow managed to jump clear; but Trina's father, heaving at the head, was knocked sideways and fetched up on his back halfway down the slope. The prow slipped round and down and ended wedged upright by the small landslide it had caused. Rearing up in the faint light from the street, it looked as though it had suddenly sprung to life.

"I've jiggered my arm," Trina's father said. "I can't move it."

"I'll take the prow. Where do you want it to go?"

"Goodness knows," Trina's father said. He was clutching his shoulder and his face was drawn with pain. "The shed's gone. You couldn't manage it alone anyway."

"I could though," Sparrow replied. "Things aren't heavy when I fly."

"I believe you could," Trina's father gasped, as he tried to struggle into a sitting position. He closed his eyes. "Rainbow lights," he muttered. "Rainbow lights before my eyes." His forehead was beaded with sweat.

"Do you remember the rainbow?" said Sparrow. " Before I was properly here, and I tried to fly? The shed and the mountain?"

Trina's father seemed barely conscious. "Take it there," he murmured. "Yes. Good place."

"I think that's the answer," said Sparrow seriously. "But would you be all right here, if I left you?"

Trina's father didn't answer.

Sparrow hesitated. Which was more important, the injured man, or the dragon-prow? Trina's father seemed to have fainted, which must mean that his injured arm was bad. On the other hand, all Mother Egg had said to do was to find the missing piece of the boat. But she hadn't said he was to do anything *with* it. He rose into the air and flew to the prow, then worked it loose and pulled. It came free easily, and Sparrow hovered there holding it as if it were no heavier than one of the feathery dragon bones, though it hung below him to three times his height. He didn't even know the way to the mountain from here.

At that moment, people came round the corner of the buildings on the far side of the street. There were three or four of them. Sparrow didn't think they looked dangerous. "Over here!" he called. "There's a man hurt! Help! Please!"

He remembered Kittel once telling him that people in the city didn't always help you if you were in trouble, but these people started to come towards the building site as soon as Sparrow shouted to them. He wasted no more time. "I hope I'll see you again," he said to Trina's father, and rose swiftly up into the black air. He heard shouts below him, but he paid no heed, and the city with its necklaces of lights and great scabs of burning buildings fell away beneath him.

As soon as he was high enough to be clear of the lights, Sparrow found himself under a paling sky scattered with a few stars. The deep roar of the city, the smell of burning, faded.

Almost straight away he saw the mountain. Or, rather, he saw where the mountain was. There was never a moment's doubt about it. There was a light, like the light that filled the Scroll Cupboard, only brighter, which drew his attention – a pale silver fire that burned far, far off in the dark west, yet which drew him like a beacon. He flew slowly towards it, hampered by the bulky timber wrapped in his arms.

The swift dawn was coming up behind him, and gradually the beacon fire ahead seemed to be getting paler. Before long he could see the grey outline of the pyramid-shaped mountain he had seen from the Scroll Cupboard. Closer and closer he flew, while the pale fire faded, until he was circling over it. And then he saw the wreck of the aeroplane, and understood.

Had Puckel planned all this? How had things actually happened? Puckel had removed and shrunk a mountain-top; an aeroplane had crashed onto the flat-topped remains of the mountain; Sparrow had thrown the shrunken mountain-top through a hole in the Hollywell; it had grown back to its original size; an aeroplane had crashed onto it.

As he circled downwards, the mountain below him seemed to get smaller, greener. It was no longer the great mountain he had seen from the Scroll Cupboard, but the small green hill he had landed on when he first came through from the Hollywell. There was a white line, like a thread, disappearing and reappearing among the trees on the slopes of the hill; and there were people, walking up and down near to the white line. Where should the dragon-prow go? He could see the old railway shed now, just across the dark line of a small river at the foot of the hill. Would he be seen if he flew down there just now?

Then he understood that he could land nowhere else but on the top of the hill. The light had guided him there. The proud dragon-prow didn't belong in a dusty old shed. It should stand on the hilltop. He stooped down the morning-wind towards it.

And as he came closer, the pale fire, which had almost disappeared, suddenly blazed up towards him in a sheet of flame. He cried out, and threw his arms across his eyes, dropping the prow as he did so. It fell out of sight into the dazzling silver light. He rose again, but as he rose the silver fire chased upwards until he seemed to be held, like the point of a candle-flame, at the tip of the light. And at that moment the sun rose.

20

THROUGH THE BARRIER

Trina ran. The dog was forgotten and the old woman was forgotten. For a short while, the thought had passed through her mind that the whole business with the dog had just been a miserable trick by the old crone – a trick to land her in deep trouble. Now, that and every other thought was gone, and she ran for her life.

Of course, she couldn't be sure that anyone was actually chasing her. She knew that the people howling and yelling, and the people wielding knives and bottles and stones and sticks, the people running away and the people running after them, were nothing to do with her; but did *they* know that?

She ran, and occasionally she whimpered, "Dad," or sometimes even, "Mum," as she dodged in and out, keeping her eyes peeled for dark streets, dark corners, quiet places – the very places she would have avoided on a normal night. She had no idea where she was or where she was going, and still less idea where the others had got to. She ran.

There seemed to be a lull in the uproar. Trina slipped into a doorway and leaned against a tall plate-glass window, her heart hammering, her breath rough and salty. There were the remains of a glass door next to her, hanging off its hinges, shattered all over the floor. Was it safe to go on? She peered out.

No! People were surging down the street in her direction, leaping in the air, some of them banging on what looked like dustbin lids. She stepped out of the doorway to begin running again – and stopped, and gaped, despite herself, despite the danger.

The street was blocked at the other end by a flock of goats. They weren't very distinct, but she could see beards wagging and tall horns sweeping. They were goats, just like in her dreams in the hospital.

Bang – bang – bang! came from behind her. The leaping people were coming closer. Were they going to fight with the goats? *Beh – beh!* the goats answered. Heads were lowered, horns were tossed, the leader reared up on its hind legs and curvetted. Trina turned.

There was only the doorway. She slipped inside, stepping gingerly under the jagged glass that still hung from the steel frame, crunched over more broken glass in the dark interior, and crouched in the shadows.

For a long while nothing happened. She relaxed a bit and her breathing calmed down. She glanced round her. There was something familiar about the great empty hall she was in; she had been here before. The Scroll Cupboard? No – no, of course not. That door there... Then she remembered – she was in the museum.

A crash, the sound of falling glass, sudden yells, and Trina was running again, running inwards now, into the depths of the building, running blindly, not pausing to look back. There was a dim gleam of glass cases. Jagged outlines here and there where some of them were broken. Her feet crunched. It wouldn't do to fall here. She must find somewhere among all these rows of glass cabinets, somewhere to crouch and be safe till the morning came. There was a sound of running feet – of scuffling, hard feet. Was it people? There was a sound of voices – not words; voices, voices crying, wailing, gibbering, moaning. She had heard that before, in some brown nightmare darkness... She halted. Faint light had caught something ahead of her – a gleaming post, and a pale rope, about the level of her waist. Darkness beyond. A picture that had appeared before, in front of her closed eyes, appeared again in that darkness, the stooping brown mummy-figure sitting examining its empty insides. The back of her neck prickled.

She looked back. There were faint lights bobbing, like will-o'-the-wisps among the glass cases. There were whisperings, and a faint *bleh!*

At least the mummy was dark. It reflected no light. But it was dead – a dead thing – a dead person! She couldn't do it. Yet even as she told herself she couldn't do it, Trina was slipping under the rope. Her head felt as if it were full of spikes, there was a buzzing in her ears like a swarm of bees, cold sweat was running down her back, but her shaking legs were carrying her step by step into the darkness. Her hands touched the cold bony hands clasped round the bony knees. She crouched, wormed her head and shoulders under, in, up, into the huge emptiness of the ribcage...

Darkness fell; complete darkness, without a hint of light, without the shadow of a shadow. There was no feeling of being anywhere; she could as well have been floating, or flying, or falling. She closed her eyes to keep out the darkness.

Then she felt she was being held. Was it the mummy? It felt bony, whoever it was, but maybe not quite hard and bony enough... A moment later she realized that the faint shaking she could feel was herself sobbing. Who was holding her? She opened her eyes.

Somebody was hugging her, but she was looking over the somebody's shoulder at a blue triangle. She blinked, and sobbed; blinked and sobbed.

The blue triangle was a sort of doorway, and the blue was pale blue sky... Two hands took hold of her shoulders, she was pushed backwards a step. She was looking into the face of Mother Egg, thin, solemn, and faraway as ever.

"Come," said Mother Egg, and stooping she turned and passed through the triangle-shaped doorway.

"*Miaow*," said a voice from the shadows. She peered round. She seemed to be inside a very small hut. Then, near the doorway, she made out the bushy ruff and erect tail that had once been so familiar to her. "Hello, Cat," she murmured, going down on her hands and knees...

"Is that your sister?" Bull whispered, his voice hoarse and loud in the silence of the mountain-top.

But Kittel went on staring at the girl who had crawled through the doorway of the bright-painted building and was standing blinking stupidly in the pale light. There had been few days, over the last three years, when Kittel had not thought a little about her young sister. Especially at night, just before she went to sleep, she would imagine the faces of her family swimming before her eyes – Mum, Dad, Trina… Now, suddenly, everything seemed to have changed. She shook her head. "I – I don't know," she said. "I don't think I ever had a sister."

"Not quite true," Mother Egg remarked. "You have many sisters, as you would see if you could read some of the more complex scrolls. The souls of the earth are joined by many invisible threads. Human sisters, animal sisters, plant sisters, and a whole crowd of sisters in the unseen world – ghosts, sprites, angels. Brothers too. Do not underestimate the size of your family!"

"I don't know what you mean," Kittel murmured.

"You look different," Bull suddenly said to her.

"I feel different," she said, a little crossly.

"No – I mean, you look different," Bull persisted. "Your hair's darker or something. More like…" He turned towards the other girl.

The other girl was no longer there. Apart from the four of them – Puckel and Mother Egg, now sitting in the entrances of two buildings next door to each other, and Kittel and Bull – the Enclosure was quite empty.

"I've had a split personality," Kittel said. "I must have been a bit mad, after all."

"Don't be foolish," said Mother Egg sharply.

"You have been engaged in a work of great precision."

"A bridge has one foot in each of the two places it joins, that's all," Puckel put in, nodding with satisfaction.

"The mountain is in two places," Mother Egg said, "but it is one mountain. The flying ship – " she glanced briefly over towards the wrecked aeroplane – "is in two places, but it is all the one machine. This is the place where you entered the door, both now and three years ago. Now I will tell you what has been, and what will come."

"But not you, my lad," Puckel butted in, looking at Bull, who was still gaping at Kittel. "You've got a job to do. Go on, through that door – " he indicated the empty doorway of the building next to his – "and we'll meet up with you directly. Don't worry. You're a dragon-holder again, just as you were once before, and just as this one here has been –" he nodded towards Kittel – "but you'll come through, no fear of that."

Bull immediately did as he was told, crouching to go through the low entrance. The sky was beginning to shine with gold over the north-eastern mountains. Sunrise was very close. The decorated fronts of the five wooden buildings already looked as bright as if they were standing in full sunlight.

"Now I will tell you," Mother Egg began.

212

"Many years ago—"

"Five," Puckel interrupted her.

"Five hundred, more like," she retorted.

"Split the difference," Puckel said with a shrug. "Call it fifty."

"As you wish," Mother Egg said stiffly. "Many years ago, a group of children were brought here to safety. You've heard that story."

"The children on the train – during the air raids?" Kittel asked.

"Those ones," Mother Egg nodded. "But it was not the fire from the sky that was the greatest threat. They were brought to be safe from the poison of the dragon's breath. The dragon's breath had poisoned half the peoples of the world. They were hopelessly mad. Those children were brought here, and looked after until they were old enough to look after themselves. There was nothing special about them; they were not particularly clever, or strong, or talented, or virtuous. They were children of the earth such as there have always been. They lived, and they did one thing which was of great value – they learned not to ask questions. Sometimes that can be a good thing.

"Meanwhile, life in the world they had left went on. Thoughts were thought, and things were made. Some of those thoughts and things came here, though their use was not known. Time went by, and we waited while the ones ripened who would take part in the building of the bridge.

"But this little dragon – " Mother Egg smiled mysteriously at Kittel – "has been the bridge itself. Where Sparrow could only hop like a bird from one side to the other, this little dragon was split in two, and had to be made whole."

She was silent, but as she said the word "whole", a thousand little memories seemed to fall into place, all together, in Kittel's mind – Kittel, who understood at last that she was also Trina. She thought with amazement, and a little sorrow, of the years she had spent wishing she could see her father and mother and Trina again; of Trina's longing to be one of the four friends of her dreams. All that time she had been longing for what she already had. Little thoughts and memories drifted past – the growing hill on the Market Glass road, the stone in Sparrow's hand...

"If you two are quite finished now," Puckel's voice broke in, "sunrise has come and it's time we were on our way."

"Don't you think she deserved an explanation?" Mother Egg asked him sharply.

"She certainly never stops asking questions," Puckel humphed. "Just as well she wasn't one of the ones we brought here in the first place. Between her and that Bull the whole scheme would have been wrecked before we'd even had time to think it up."

"We will go," said Mother Egg, and rising from her doorway she crossed to the one next to it, the one nearly opposite Puckel's. Puckel got up and followed her, ushering on Kittel-Trina – who was trying to think which name she liked best, or whether she should just content herself with her full name of Katrina.

Following Mother Egg into the dark entrance of the doorway, she felt the sudden burst of light behind her as the sun rose; and the next moment they were standing in a place which the Kittel part of her had never seen before but which the Trina part immediately recognized – the Scroll Cupboard, lit now not by its usual dim silver light but made radiant, rich-coloured as the five painted buildings on the mountain-top, by the full light of day.

21

THE WRONG DIRECTION

Lissie and Ormand had not finished filling up the pit again when the search party returned, straggling tiredly down the ridge at the eastern end of the valley.

"I don't want to be around when they come through here," Ormand said. "I can't be bothered with all their questions."

"We won't be able to pack up and get away in time. And, anyway, we haven't finished," Lissie pointed out. "We could hide in the wood, but they'd easily find us if they wanted to."

It was very early in the morning. Their cooking-fire had been got going and was boiling up the water for their breakfast of biscuit-porridge. They were doing a little gentle filling-in to get the chill from their limbs while they waited for it. The ponies had just started on their early graze. It would certainly not be easy to disappear.

As they stood there, indecisive, a shout came – not from the men, but from the opposite direction, the west – a shout that was sudden, and echoing, and that grew in strength as it echoed. The branches of the birch wood across the stream suddenly bent as if a gust of wind had hit them. Ormand and Lissie turned, and saw a small dark figure among the trees. "That's Bull," said Lissie.

There was another great shout: "This way! Make haste! Make haste!" The echoes rolled around the valley like a rumble of stones on a dry hillside.

"That can't be Bull," Ormand said. "He could never shout like that." Yet even he had to admit that it looked like Bull coming towards them. "Let's go and see," he said.

"I don't think I want to," Lissie muttered, following him slowly.

Lissie saw Ormand reach Bull just as Plato Smithers and the others at the head of the search party came out from among the trees. The men were running. Bull stopped, as if waiting. He seemed to be ignoring Ormand. Lissie felt more and more reluctant to go up to him, yet her feet kept moving her forwards.

Bull was gazing past Ormand towards the eastern end of the valley. Lissie wasn't even sure he was looking towards the men of the villages. "What's wrong with him?" she whispered to Ormand as she came up.

"I don't know," Ormand whispered back. "Something. He won't speak to me."

"Bull?" Lissie said hesitantly.

"Make haste!" the great voice boomed out again from Bull, and the force of it sent Ormand and Lissie staggering back. Bull started to walk straight towards the clump of nettles in the middle of the valley.

"His ankle's better," Ormand remarked.

"I wish Sparrow was here," Lissie said.

"Haste!" Bull called. "I have found it!"

Now the men of the villages were coming up from the stream towards the nettle-patch. They were walking rapidly, heads down, packed together shoulder to shoulder. Like a flock of sheep, Lissie thought. But she too, although she would have liked to hang back, was following Bull. She couldn't seem to help it. Ormand was walking beside her, looking pale and tense. They came together, Ormand and Lissie facing the men of the villages across the nettles while Bull walked straight into the tall plants as if they weren't there and stood still. He was peering intently at something at his feet.

"You found it then, young Bull," said Plato Smithers, in a strained voice, as though he were trying hard to act as if everything was normal. "Leg's better too, I'm glad to see."

Then Bull raised his head and gazed round at them all. Lissie's heart missed a beat, and she almost choked on her breath. His eyes were rolled upwards, with only the whites showing. His dark face was quite expressionless.

And suddenly, with a bellow that shook loose the rocks high in the mountain crags and sent everyone staggering to their knees, the dragon came. Out of nowhere it seemed to come. One moment Bull was standing there with his blank white eyes; the next, there was no sign of him, but the huge head of the dragon was where he had been, with the vast, green-golden bulk of its body stretching back towards the western end of the valley.

They had just got to their feet when they were toppled again – this time by a small earth-quake. The dragon had dug its smoking snout into the ground – deep in, as if the ground were no more solid than water. And then, as if the dragon had simply peeled back a layer of the world to reveal another, in place of the Valley of Murmuring Water they were standing on the short turf by the huge, still trees of the Holly-well in Ormand's own garden.

Ormand and Lissie blinked. Everything was as they had left it two weeks before. And every-thing else was as it had been two minutes before – the dragon, the bewildered men of the five villages – but for no more than a second. Again the dragon bellowed, and the glossy spiked leaves shivered down in a shower out of the holly trees. Again the snout plunged into the earth, and the ground that was Lissie and Ormand's home was ripped apart.

And they were in a wild, rocky place, surrounded on three sides by a towering cliff. Ormand and Lissie quickly recognized it as the place called the Echoing Hall just outside the village of Springing Wood.

Again a roar – and this time the blast of the dragon's voice rebounded from all sides of the cliff so that they were deafened and dizzied by the din, and everything went black before their eyes – and a third time the terrible head plunged into the rock. And as it did so, the sun rose into a cleft in the rock face and shone through on them.

22

THE MOMENT OF DANGER

Because everything happened so quickly, Kittel found it impossible to say whether she and Puckel and Mother Egg had arrived before the dragon, or whether the dragon had arrived before them, or whether they had all arrived together. At any rate, there the dragon was, lying across the floor of the Scroll Cupboard while its tail snaked away down one wall. Its head and shoulders lay in an arch-shaped opening in the opposite wall, and right in front of its nose stood Ormand and Lissie – Ormand nearer to it, pale and terrified, Lissie huddling behind him – with their backs to a glorious, shining thing that Kittel knew must be Sparrow's bridge. Clustered round the dragon's tail were twenty bewildered-looking village men, while crawling on hands and knees on the sandy ground beside its immense flank was

Bull, looking very sick and shaky.

No one moved. Two long wisps of smoke issued from the dragon's nostrils and bent in a slight breeze that came from the wide sky and the distant world outside. Kittel wondered how long it took for the dragon's breath to send you mad.

"Aren't you going to do something?" she whispered to Puckel. Puckel ignored her. She could see no sign of Mother Egg.

Then the dragon spoke – a soft, hissing sound quite unlike the thunderous bellow which was the only sound Kittel had heard from it before. It was almost a sweet sound, thin, vague, a little like the sound of wind in trees. "Son of a slug," it said, "daughter of earthworms, you are standing between me and my bridge. What have you to say?"

Its great jaws scarcely moved, but at each word a thick puff of smoke shot upwards from its nostrils. It was almost as if it were speaking through its nose. Kittel saw Ormand's mouth working. Lissie was staring back at the dragon over Ormand's shoulder, her normally ruddy face pale as a toadstool. Then Ormand gave several great gulps, and spoke.

"I don't think it's really your bridge," he stammered. "Sparrow made it, you see ... it was out of the bones of another dragon ... we dug them up."

There was a small explosion of smoke from

the dragon's jaws, and a broad, indistinct noise, like a gale getting up in the distance. It occurred to Kittel that the dragon was laughing.

"What do you know of bones?" the great beast said. "You understand nothing. Step aside."

Kittel noticed now that, although the narrow end of the shining bridge rested on the floor of the Scroll Cupboard, just behind Lissie's feet there was a gap in it where it began its huge, impossible arch into empty air. She could see nothing below the bridge, which scarcely looked solid and had no parapet or rail, and she could only pray that Lissie wouldn't step back.

But now Lissie was mumbling something into Ormand's ear. "No," Ormand said after she had finished, his voice scarcely louder than a whisper. "No, I think we've just got to stay here." Ormand looked both determined and uncertain. Kittel realized he had not noticed her and Puckel.

"You have strayed into my dream, slug-son," the dragon said. "Yet I am awake. When you dug your impudent blade into the soil of my resting place, you strayed in then. Now you are trapped, like these sheep at my tail. Look – "

And suddenly the whole scene was reversed. Ormand and Lissie stood inside the Scroll Cupboard, while the dragon lay facing them with its tail stretched across the bridge, its neck bridging the gap. "What do you say now,

223

little ones?" it hissed.

Again, Lissie murmured into Ormand's ear. "I say – " Ormand brought the words out with a struggle – "that dragons can't go backwards!"

"Ha!" the dragon's voice was for a moment like an echo of its terrifying bellow, while an even bigger gout of brown smoke burst upwards. A second later the scene was as it had been before – Ormand and Lissie with their backs to the bridge, the dragon stretched across the floor of the Scroll Cupboard.

"Give me back something of what you've taken," came the dragon's soft hiss, "and I'll let you go free."

"I don't think we can," said Ormand. "I was only doing what I was told, and we weren't supposed to touch the bones. It was an accident, and I think that's why the bridge—"

The dragon cut him short. "What have you in your hand?" it hissed.

"Nothing," Ormand replied.

"Let me see this nothing," the dragon said.

Bewildered, Ormand opened his hand, palm toward the dragon.

"It is, indeed, a very small nothing," the dragon hissed agreeably. "Hold it closer, so that I may see it better."

Ormand obediently stretched his hand further out towards the dragon.

"Closer still," the dragon sighed. "The

nothing is almost invisible."

Ormand stepped towards the dragon, holding his hand out at full stretch.

Snap! A sound like cracking rock split the air. The dragon lunged forward. A second later there was a piercing scream from Lissie. "Ormand! Your arm! Oh no, your arm!"

Ormand dropped to his knees, clutching at his right shoulder. But there was nothing to clutch; his arm was clean away, chopped off just below the shoulder. There was no blood, no mess – just the stump of an arm that looked as though it might have healed years ago.

At that moment, Bull staggered to his feet, lurched forward, and supporting himself against the dragon's crooked foreleg, then its huge jaw, stumbled to the edge of the bridge, almost brushing the dragon's nose. He seized Ormand by his remaining arm and dragged him clear, back towards Puckel. It was perhaps the bravest thing he had ever done, though in fact the dragon paid no attention. Lissie, both hands clapped over her mouth as if to stop herself screaming again, tottered after them. Whether or not they had been able to see Puckel before, they could clearly see him now.

"Why didn't you stop it?" Kittel found herself sobbing, shaking Puckel by the arm as she sobbed. "I asked you to do something." She felt weak and sick.

"A price had to be paid," the old man said,

taking hold of Ormand's shoulders and steadying him on his feet. He was now holding his stick in his hand. "Well done," he said. And then, "Look – here comes the young one."

Kittel was so used to Sparrow flying that the first thing she did was glance up into the air. But Sparrow was not flying; he was walking slowly towards them over the glittering bridge.

In fact, it was only the long curve of the bridge's arch that made him look as though he was coming slowly; he was actually walking quite quickly, with a light, confident step and a strange air about him as if he had just discovered everything that there was to know about anything. He was dressed in the old, shabby, patched clothes that boys in the mountain villages always wore. Kittel and Trina compared notes about him: Trina told Kittel that this was not Pats; Kittel told Trina that this was Sparrow; Trina and Kittel agreed that Sparrow and Pats looked very alike but were not exactly alike; both of them wondered who, or what, Pats had been, all those years when Sparrow was living his life in the mountains. "Sparrow ought to be in Pats' clothes," Trina told Kittel. "Illusion," Kittel told Trina. "Clothes are just an illusion – Sparrow can make mountains look like clouds..."

Sparrow came without hesitation to the edge of the bridge, and stood with the toes of his boots just poking over into the gap between him and the first two dragon bones. The dragon crouched, eyeing him intently. He faced it straight-on and said, "Here I am."

"I know," said the dragon, in a smooth, long-drawn whisper like a wind in the keyhole of a door. "And can you come any further?"

"Not while you're there," Sparrow answered promptly. He was looking into its orange-smouldering eyes without any sign of fear.

The dragon spoke again. "Would you like to have the bridge completed, little Puka?" it said softly.

"Yes, I would," said Sparrow.

"I could make it complete, but you must step out of my way."

"Then it would be finished for you, but not for me," Sparrow said carefully.

"That is true," the dragon answered, with a low laugh like the echo of an owl's wings amongst rocks. There was a long silence.

"Will Sparrow be safe?" Kittel whispered anxiously to Puckel. "The dragon could just frazzle him up, couldn't it?"

"Not here," Puckel replied. "Not in the Scroll Cupboard, where the names of all living things are kept – here nothing can kill. The dragon can't move forward across the bridge if a living soul stands in his way. Watch, and listen."

"I will make a bargain with you," the dragon said to Sparrow.

"All right," said Sparrow warily.

"Let me ask you a question," the dragon hissed. "If you cannot answer it, the bridge is for me to use; if you answer it correctly, it is for you to use – a living bridge, or a bridge of bones."

Sparrow glanced over at Puckel. But Puckel's face was as set as a statue's. "All right," Sparrow said at last.

"How are things, in the scrumptious little world down there?" the dragon asked.

"Is that the question?" said Sparrow.

"No," said the dragon, "I was merely being conversational."

"There's burning. There's fighting. I think they're all crazy there."

"Still!" the dragon exclaimed, with another of its long, husky laughs. "Then all is ripe for my return, and my eager little flock –" the monster's eyes rolled back towards the men of the five villages – "will be the first to cross and see what they've been missing for so long."

"You didn't like it much last time you were there."

"Ha!" said the dragon, as a gout of black smoke shot up from it like an umbrella. "This is the question, little Puka. Listen. This will put the grin on the back of your head."

Sparrow, who had not been grinning at all, began to look extremely serious.

"It is this," said the dragon. "Are the things

in the world there because I dream them; or do I dream them because they are there?"

"That's the question it asked you!" Kittel whispered frantically to Puckel. "Do you know the answer now?"

"I do," said Puckel, never taking his eyes off Sparrow.

"Can't you tell Sparrow?" Kittel asked.

"No, I can't," Puckel answered curtly.

"Why not? It's life or death – it might be the end of the world!"

"I can't tell him," Puckel retorted, "because the question has no answer."

Kittel looked round desperately. There must be something they could do! She looked at the stick in Puckel's hand. Couldn't she grab it, and throw it over to Sparrow, or something? But the stick looked back at her very woodenly. I am nothing but a stick, it seemed to be saying, there's no point in looking at me. Then she looked over at Sparrow again, in sudden doubt. A memory – Trina's memory – flitted through her mind. The riddle ... the riddle that had no answer...

Sparrow had not been grinning before, but he was now. A broad smile of self-satisfaction was on his face. He rocked himself gently backwards and forwards at the edge of the awesome abyss.

"You must tell me something before you hear the answer to that, Ureychyoburenitho," he said.

"What must I tell you?" the dragon hissed.

"You must tell me who you're asking," Sparrow said calmly.

"Why you, boy – you! Who else?" the dragon growled.

"Not so fast," said Sparrow. "I've been in and out of so many shapes, I just don't know who I am any more. Are you asking a boy you're dreaming of because he's there – or a boy who's there because you're dreaming of him?"

There was an awful silence. The smoke that seeped from the dragon's jaws grew slowly thicker. Yet as it grew thicker, it also became paler. From black to brown it turned, and from brown to gold, and from gold to white. Sparrow's form could only dimly be seen now, swathed in the drifting cloud. And then from white, the smoke turned to colours – yellow and green and blue, and then a luminous violet like cranesbill flowers. And still Sparrow was there, upright in front of the dragon.

Slowly the smoke cleared, until only two thin wisps were rising from the beast's nostrils.

"I have bones in my mouth, little Puka," the dragon said.

"Let's have them then," said Sparrow. "It's time we were off for our breakfast."

The massive, tooth-spiked jaws of the dragon opened, its black tongue flicked, something shot into the air which Sparrow caught in his hand. For a moment, Kittel, Bull, Ormand and

Lissie glimpsed a white bone, with a joint in the middle and a small fan-shape at the end, which must once have been Ormand's arm and hand – and then Sparrow bent and placed it under his toes.

The Scroll-Cupboard, the abyss of sky, the rainbow bridge and the world at its foot, the dragon and the men of the five villages – all vanished without a sound and without a trace. The young people were standing in the sunlight under a blue sky alive with huge white clouds. Their ears were filled with an endless, musical, booming roar. They were on a mountain, flat-topped but empty, scattered with outcrops of gleaming white-and-gold rock. The largest of these, just beside them, reared up like stone clouds, and on the top sat Puckel, cross-legged and still, with Mother Egg behind him.

Then they looked down and saw the waterfall. It poured from a gap under the rocks where Puckel sat, foamed wildly over the broken ground at the mountain's edge, and fell, thousands of feet it seemed, gathering in strength and power as it fell, deep blue-green, bearded with white foam, casting rainbow shadows over the whole mountainside. They had never seen a waterfall so huge or so beautiful, not even Kittel and Sparrow, who had once seen something like a copy of this one. From the cliff-top, they could see the whole of their mountain-country stretching below in its humped and jagged and pinnacled glory, green valleys and the grey bones of mountainsides, deep-cleft rivers and snow-gleaming peaks.

"King Puck," said Sparrow in awe. "We've come to King Puck. It doesn't seem like a hidden place, but I could never find it."

"Now you will be able to find it at all times," Puckel said. "For I am going to have a well-earned rest, but you'll be needing my advice pretty soon, I expect, and I shall be here to give it. You'll have your work cut out with that bridge. You must learn how to come and go across it, and you will have to teach your whole troop how to do the same."

"What troop?" said Sparrow.

"Well, what do you think that school's for? The men of the five villages? Not likely! You need younger fools, tender ones, still able to bend. You didn't think this was the end of it all and you could just go back to fishing and pony-trekking, did you? There's work to be done – serious work, grim work. The Polymorphs have kicked up a rare old rumpus for you down there; that'll cause you problems, though it's to help you in the long run. A smoke screen to work behind.

"So, listen, all of you. You are the first. You are the teachers, you are the leaders. All have your places, all have your tasks. You are a seed, just as the top of this mountain is a seed, planted by Sparrow on the other side of the bridge. Don't expect to see results, mind. Healing will take a long time, and there's only so much you can do in one lifetime. We have made a chink in the armour of the sorry world beyond the bridge, and it will be for you to pour the first of the power of the Giants' Door through that chink. No more goats now; things can be more direct – you will be little goats yourselves. Many goats – and a Sparrow, and a Cat, and a Bull."

He turned to Bull. "Bulls are too big to cross," he said. "You must learn to grow smaller, boy. It will be a long task. You will be needed to direct and govern things among the people of the five villages. No more wild-goose chases off into the mountains! But when you do cross, you will go as the representative of the dragon – as Kittel came here as the representative of the dragon. Through Bull the dragon will cross the bridge, but will no longer be able to break out of Bull's form."

Bull looked doubtful.

"Don't worry, boy," Puckel said. "You will have great power. That's what you've always wanted. It's not always a bad thing. But Sparrow will have you in the palm of his hand, and that's the best place for you to be. Together you'll do great things, take my word for it. And now, old spindle-shanks – "

Suddenly he turned round and seized

Mother Egg by the ankle. Dumbfounded, they watched the old lady being lifted off the ground and turned unceremoniously upside down by Puckel, until her head was on the ground beside them. She didn't protest and she seemed to have gone quite rigid. Puckel put both hands on the soles of her feet and then vaulted off his perch on the rock to land beside them himself, and where she had been, Puckel's old stick was in his hands again.

"And now," he said briskly, "breakfast, and then a send-off. You, my dear – " he turned to Kittel – "are expected, over across the bridge, but we won't make you cross *that* on an empty stomach."

Kittel's mouth seemed to have gone dry. "You mean..." she mumbled, but couldn't bring any more words out. It was one thing, thinking of a bridge to cross to get back home, but quite another to think of that narrow shining thing, with nothing to hang on to, nothing to support her, spanning a horror of empty air...

Puckel nodded. "You'll manage," he said briefly, giving her a wink. "There's nothing worth getting that isn't worth a bit of a struggle. You'll get used to it."

"You've fallen off a cliff before," Sparrow put in with a grin. "And you're still here."

And Kittel had to be content with that.

EPILOGUE

"I didn't get a lift home with a stranger," Trina told her father. "I walked."

"You must admit it's a bit hard to believe," he said.

"Well, Mum certainly thinks I'm a liar." She fell silent. The monotonous hum of the engine, the buzz-buzz of the windscreen wipers and the hiss of tyres on wet road were the only sounds. They drove slowly, because Trina's father had his arm in a sling and it was hard for him to steer properly.

They had been to collect his things from the university. The university had been closed down because of all the damage. Its library had been burned to the ground, and now no one knew what was going to happen.

For the three days since the riot there had been almost constant, driving rain. The city was unutterably dreary – blackened buildings, streaks of soot and ash washed across walls and pavements by the rain, piles of rubble, holes in the road, burned-out cars. Everywhere there were soldiers. Dark-painted army lorries and armoured cars stood in every street. There was hardly any of the normal city traffic, and no crowds. It seemed that if more than four or five people met together, they were quickly surrounded by soldiers with guns who searched them and told them to go away home.

Trina's father seemed very depressed. "A lot of things are going to change – for the worse," he said. "It's been coming for a long time. I just hate to think what kind of world you'll be growing up in."

"'Vexed to nightmare,'" Trina said, with a small smile. It was a relief to be out of the house, away from her mother's accusing glances. And she felt light at heart.

"What's that?" her father demanded.

"'Vexed to nightmare,'" she repeated. "It's in a poem Pats' dad keeps saying."

"He's off with the fairies," her father muttered. "Always has been."

"It's not really a nightmare though," Trina said. "Whatever it looks like. It's a smoke-screen."

"I don't know what you're talking about," he said crossly.

They were coming home by the Market

Glass road. "Dad," she said suddenly. "You know when I went off – I mean the other time, for that whole week?"

"Yes?"

"I know where I was now."

"Where?"

"The same place as when I got lost in the riot."

Her father sighed. "Where was that?"

"I don't know."

"What's the point in telling me, then?"

Trina sighed. *Buzz-buzz*, *buzz-buzz*, went the windscreen wipers. Then *squeak-squeak*, *squeak-squeak*; the rain had stopped. "Dad?" she said.

"What?"

"You've not to worry."

"How can I not worry about you?"

"There's things happening," she said. "I won't be here all the time. I've work to do."

"You'll have exams before very long."

"Oh – exams," she said. She shook her head. "It won't be like that."

"If you don't do well in your exams, it'll spoil your chances in life, you know."

The conversation wasn't going the way she wanted it to go. She would never be able to talk to her parents, to tell them… But all of a sudden her father laughed. "Listen to me! I'm like an old cracked record. You'd never think half the university had just been burned down. I don't know where we're going, Kit. I don't know what things are going to be like. There's no point in coming to me for fatherly advice – about exams, or anything else."

"I know," she said. "You've just got to trust me."

The clouds were starting to break up, rolling back over the dark hills in streamers and flags. By the time they came in sight of the Stack, pale sunlight was falling in shafts on the green country. All of a sudden – "Look!" Trina said. "The rainbow!"

Out of the side of the Stack the great arch sprang, rising, shining with almost painful brightness to the height of the pewter-coloured sky, disappearing into the white sides of mountainous clouds.

"It always makes you feel better, a rainbow," her father said. "It almost looks solid, doesn't it."

"Yes, it does," Trina agreed.

MORE WALKER PAPERBACKS

For You to Enjoy